Dear
Déon

THE BOOK OF SASQUATCH

I hope you
enjoy The book.
Best Wishes!

Jno Cute
914-708-6103

THE BOOK OF
Sasquatch

LOUIS CONTE

City Bear Press
Manahawkin, New Jersey

Library of Congress Control Number: 2020949136

ISBN 978-1-7351631-9-2 (paperback)
ISBN 978-1-7351631-4-7 (e-book)

Published by City Bear Press
19 Henry Drive
Manahawkin, NJ 08050
www.citybearpress.com

Printed and bound in the
United States of America

For Thomas

"Poor Grendel's had an accident,"
I whisper. "So may you all."

—John Gardner, *Grendel*

Contents

Chapter One

AND SO BEGINS another night of my insane war against Joseph Hasselbeck and his minions from the North American Primate Research Organization. Once again, they've invaded my world and upset the delicate web of nature in my lush, forest domain. In the darkening gloom of evening, I watch intently as they prepare for their hunt.

I am what they are hunting.

I've been watching them for months. They claim to be researchers; they claim they want nothing other than to learn about me and my kind. And while I know they won't stalk me to a violent end, their intent is, nonetheless, violent. Please don't try to convince me otherwise.

Hasselbeck's team set up a base camp in a clearing at the end of a dirt road. A larger crew of men has joined them, bringing cameras and lighting equipment. The group is all geared up with flashlights, night vision goggles, parabolic listening devices, and cameras: I've heard them use these words as they worked. I don't know what these devises really do, but they say this is what they need to make a movie. And this is why they hunt me.

These researchers didn't consider that a reasonably intelligent hominid might hear a bunch of heavy-footed humans trampling through the woods in the middle of the night with a television crew? I hear every sound they make, every word, every whisper.

Piss off you weak, hairless monkeys!

I should rip their heads off and smash their skulls against a rock. Capture that on camera. That would teach them to come into my territory, my domain, my lair.

It really doesn't matter. They won't see me. They won't even get a glimpse. Oh, maybe I'll tickle their balls a little and let out a howl after they've finished their usual imitations of my shouts, grunts and tree knocks, hoping to draw me out. But please – help me get this through their thick skulls - I have no intention of actually showing myself to them.

They are beneath me.

These people have a greater chance of seeing the Thunderbird than they have of seeing me. But I will follow them to keep an eye on what they are up to. Maybe they have some new ruse that they want to roll out for the camera crew.

Hey, its entertainment for me until my night gets going.

At least these hunters didn't bring guns. It is good that they didn't. They're more likely to shoot themselves than me. There is nothing more dangerous than a human with a gun - except, perhaps, a drunken human with a gun. I've seen both. More on that later, but let me assure you that I have no intention of ending up stuffed in a dusty museum for eternity.

This war started after a human shot one of my sons. He was so young, so full of life. He would have sired a dozen little hairy ones. And now he's gone. After I committed his body to the Lake of Souls, I sent a mind-message to my elder, Shattuck the Gray. "We should kill them all."

His message back shook me. "Beyond our lands, they have vast settlements that glow in the night. They live in crowded chaos, surrounded by their machines. They are numbered like the stars."

"They can't get out of their own way. How can they be so many that I can't take revenge?"

"If you start killing them, more will come."

"How can that be?"

"Remember, we must keep our world secret."

"They killed my son."

Then the old wise left me in silence.

Humans disgust me. They kill for pleasure and destroy things of value. They pollute their own drinking water. They abuse and lie to each other. They even disrespect their women. And they eat too damn much.

They've lost their honor and their magic. They are a plague upon our lands.

All, except the Shaman and the wandering boy. The boy is different. I am not ready to talk about him yet.

Do I seem angry?

Actually, I'm in good spirits on this dark, summer evening in the verdant land the native humans and my people call the *Hoh*. I count my blessings as the moon rises over the mist-covered mountains. I've eaten well today - some salmon and some green onions. And a lovely little lady from over the ridge has signaled that she's ready and willing. Why not? I am the dominant one in this stretch of wilderness. And when a woman signals to come on over, well, you go. Yes, our time together will be brief but productive. One must seize the chance to create new life. Eleven months from now there will be a new crumb snatcher clinging to her breasts. I will move on but provide protection from afar as I do for all my women and little ones. We will pass each other silently from time to time. Our eyes glowing, knowingly, until the next time...

It is our way.

We are not like you. Do not believe for a moment that our silence means aloneness. We are few, but we are connected through time and blood.

The strapping Hasselbeck and his crew are slogging up a trail toward me, the glare of their lights invading the woods. Every animal in the region knows they are here. That would include the elusive primates these idiots are trying to film.

Oh, the large hunter named *Mongo* slipped and fell into some mud. Ha ha! Hee hee! Did you boys get that on film?

They get to the top of a rise, don their night vision glasses, and scan the horizon as the camera crew films. The Big Foot hunters look magnificent. And it is very dramatic.

They see nothing, of course.

If you are blind to the reality of the world around you, technology will not help you to see it.

But the fun is about to start.

"Eeoohh," Hasselbeck bellows into the night. Across the valley, another human male shouts, *"Waaaah!"*

Yeah, right. That's what I sound like. Laughable.

Wham! Wham! Mongo whacks a tree with a piece of wood because he believes my kind communicate that way. They stand still with audio equipment, intently listening for my response.

What a bunch of bear-turds.

But I can't help myself. I throw a large rock into the woods twenty feet off the trail. It lands with a loud thump.

"I think one threw a rock into the woods!" Hasselbeck whispers excitedly into his radio.

"One threw a rock?" Mongo replies.

Hasselbeck pumps his fist. "That was amazing!"

Amazing, my ass, you annoying troll. It was a rock thrown in the woods - nothing more than that. I've propelled rocks that crushed a deer's skull from a hundred feet away. *That* was amazing. And I got some meat, too. I should've put the rock through your forehead, Hasselbeck. I would bet that the camera man would have freaked out as he filmed your brains and shattered skull splattering into the mud.

But then I would have angered Shattuck. You shouldn't anger your elders.

"Let's do another tree knock." Wham! Wham!

"Again!" Wham! Wham!

Silence. Let them eat silence.

Why not show myself and be done with it? I should lower myself from my high perch and reveal myself to these primitives? They are just seeking discovery you say?

I have seen one of their other primate "discoveries" now trapped behind bars in the small zoo at the edge of the wilderness, staring blankly at the humans passing by, begging for food, mugging for the cameras. I have seen this "discovery," defeated and pathetic, his spirit and magic gone - a slave for the amusement of the gawking humans who live on the edge of our lands.

And I know what happened to the native humans when the people from the East discovered them. "Discovery" often opens the gate to slaughter.

Hasselbeck and his fellow researchers will have a *discovery* when they get back to their vehicles. For shits and giggles, I stuffed half a pine tree into the cabin of Hasselbeck's truck. And then I ripped open their food containers and ate some provisions. I left garbage all over their camp site. Rachel, the skeptical, athletic female researcher, will argue that it was evidence of a bear. Even though we all know that bears don't stuff trees into cars.

And they shall debate my existence.

"It was a bear!"

"It was a Squatch!"

"There's not enough proof."

And so it goes.

There is not enough proof of me. There is no proof of us. Humans will never discover us because they don't know how to look and don't know how to listen. We have evolved ways of avoiding and deceiving people over the vast expanse of time.

We understood you long before you understood you. And we didn't need technology or scientists. We are wise in ways beyond your comprehension.

We were here first.

So there will be the occasional foot print or blurry photograph. The rare encounter which most won't even report. And if you do get something noteworthy, we can count on your envy, greed, and jealousy to make what is clear, opaque. Someone will want credit for "the discovery." Other hunters will wallow in envy. Words like *hoax* and *fringe kook* will marginalize or discredit those who figure us out. And then you will go back to your money and machines.

As I said, we understand you.

I would rather die than be discovered. I shall remain a myth, full of power and magic. The native humans worship me like a God. They call me *the wild man, the hairy brother, C'iatqo.*

I am Sasquatch, protector of the Lake of Souls.

Spirit of the Dark Woods.

Chapter Two

I'VE ALWAYS LEANED toward the melancholy. I admit it. I tend to brood. But the women love the strong silent types, particularly when they're bigger than two bears and can rip a leg off a bull moose and beat him to death with it. Nothing says, "Now this one's got some serious genetic potential," better than presenting a lovely lady with some fresh moose meat.

And that's what I should have been doing that early summer day when instead I was standing at the edge of the forest staring at the primate in the cage at the county zoo. The few humans who visit the place were gone. A grey-haired human male in a white coat had just poked the orange-haired primate with some sort of needle. The ape accepted the jab without protest. He now loafed on the branch of an artificial tree made of cement and plastic leaves in the middle of his "Orang-utan Habitat Enclosure."

Yes, I can read your words. I know that you think and function with words. Words, words, words, as though that makes you special.

I glared down at this ape from a hill in the woods that

ended forty feet from his enclosure. Enclosure - meaning *enclosed*. As in *not free to leave* to go climb a real tree and look for some orange-haired females, which I've never seen around these parts, but, whatever.

Tang looked so stupid and pathetic - sitting on an imitation tree in the middle of a forest. I just couldn't take my eyes off him. Could he mind speak?

"Tang," I messaged.

Silence.

"Tang."

Nothing.

I threw a small rock at him. It hit him on the foot.

"What did you do that for?"

Ah, so orange hair could mind-talk!

"I've been trying to get your attention, you orange-haired fool."

"Attention is greatly over-valued around these parts."

"That's the problem. You've accepted your situation. You need to stand up to the hairless ones. You should toss feces at the human when he jabs you."

"Dr. Orenstein gave me my medicine."

"Are you sick?"

"No. But they say I need it."

"I think the white-coated Orenstein ought to give you a check-up from the neck up. You should've bitten his fingers off."

"But they feed me."

"So what? You're a captive, a slave, an entertainment for these slugs. When night falls, I'll rip the cage apart and free you."

"Oh, I don't want that. I'm content here."

"What? How can you be content in a cage?"

"It's not so bad. They feed me well. I sleep inside at night. Once every couple of years, I get to visit females as part of the breeding program."

"A breeding-program?" I nearly pulled the hair out of

my crested skull. "You don't need their breeding program. I can't think of anything more un-natural than breeding on a schedule set by humans. Your women go along with this?"

"The women I meet have also spent their lives enclosed."

"My women would smack me with a forty-pound salmon if I tried to dictate when they're ready to rock. That's what makes it so special. You can't schedule our thing. Come with me, brother, and I will show you what love magic is all about."

The orange one rubbed his chin. "I don't understand what you mean by *magic*."

"You'll see. You can have magic again."

"I don't know what you're talking about."

"You don't know of magic? You don't know what it is to hear the minds of the others? To feel the joy of new life being born two mountains away from you? The profound loss when a venerated elder descends into the Lake of Souls? You don't know any of this?"

"No. But I get all the fruit I want and a warm place to live."

Tang clearly needed help. I needed to consult with an elder about this fellow because he was as dumb as bear scat.

And then the message came. My oldest son was in trouble. One of my women saw a hunter stalking him from a distance.

I ran through the woods faster than a bull in rut, crashing through the brush. Trees falling before me, herds of deer fleeing in terror.

A bearded white hunter was following my son, who didn't know he was being stalked. Adolescents are so reckless!

The images were flying into my brain as I swung through the trees, down a ravine. There he was! I burst into the clearing and charged him.

He fired the shot.

The image of my son falling to the ground seared through me.

I shoved the hunter and sent him flailing through the air. He slammed into a tree and crumpled to the ground. "You monster! You shot my son!" I screamed.

He writhed in agony, spitting blood. "What the hell!" he stammered, barely able to get to his knees. "My shoulder's broke. What are you?"

"You know exactly what I am! I'm going to slit your gut and rip your intestines out!"

"You can talk?!"

"Yes. So could my son. You had no right to shoot him!"

"I have the Second Amendment!" He reached for his rifle.

"You have *what*?!"

He put a round in the gun. "The right to bear arms."

"Good. Then I have the right to rip them off!"

I was upon him in the blink of an eye, clutching him by his throat, and lifting him over my head. "Ahhh!" he gagged as I turned to the edge of the ravine. I hurled him down and watched as his body slammed against rock after rock, tumbling into oblivion.

I ran to my son. My women gathered around him, moaning. He was bleeding out onto the dirt. Skeknal was kneeling, rocking back and forth, her hands rubbing his chest. She looked up at me and opened the palms of her hands. "They have destroyed my son. Bring him back to me."

I touched her hands and felt my son's blood. When our eyes met, she looked away. I went to my knees.

"I am sorry, father. I was reckless." My son fought for breath. "I left tracks after I wrestled an elk this morning. It was such fun."

I cleared the hair from his face and held him in my arms. "I know, my son. I have done that as well. It is what we do sometimes. I forgive you."

"I shall die. I know this." His eyes glowed. "I am not afraid."

I pulled him closer. "Tell me of the elk."

"He was strong and full of fight. He was...beautiful."

My son's blood dripped through my fingers. "My son, I shall lift you to the sky and announce to the Creator that one of us will be hunting in his realm. We are joined through time and blood."

Life left his eyes.

I lifted my son to the sky and the women gathered around me. Our voices joined in grief as we swayed together. We raised our arms together, holding his body high. Our grief energy merged and I let it out.

"WAAAAAHOOO!"

"WAAAAAHOOO!" the women cried.

The wilderness exploded with our cries. Mourning howls filled the sky as the moon rose into the darkening night.

The Creator had been given notice.

But I had to wonder if the Creator still existed. Had the human monsters hunted him to the brink of extinction as well?

"Take him to the Lake of Souls," Shattuck whispered to my mind. "He will be missed."

I tied rocks to my son's body with vines. As I prepared his body for the Lake of Souls, I heard Skeknal whisper a prayer to my mind.

"Go from this place of pain to where the instruments of man shall no longer torment you. Go to where we walk in peace, free and proud with our ancestors under the warmth of the blue sky. The mountains, become a part of them. The trees, become part of them. The waters, flow with them. You will flow through us, my son and live forever in our memories."

I swam with his body to the middle of the lake. There, I let him go.

I crawled out of the lake and cursed the humans.

The next day I found the hunter's mangled body at the bottom of the ravine, still clutching his gun. His head had exploded against a rock where his body came to rest. Flies buzzed about him and vultures circled hungrily above. Some crows had already been at him.

Should I bury his body? No, I decided. Let the woods and the birds take him.

I ripped the gun from his cold, dead hands and shattered it against a rock.

We should kill them all.

Chapter Three

MY MELANCHOLY TURNED to grief, my grief to anger, and my anger to hatred. I obsessed over the arrogant humans and stalked the small town of Deception Falls at the edge of my domain, vengeance burning in my heart.

From the shadows I watched them, moving about their homes, businesses, and their government buildings. I crept close at night and watched them at their places of worship, hearing them through the walls. I have ears twice the size of a humans' and I haven't lost the ability to use them. I made note of the humans who lied and cheated on their lovers. I made note of those who stole from others and those who beat their women.

One afternoon I saw a group of people carrying signs, shouting at a home at the end of a road. Although there were three houses at the end of the road, the humans were yelling at only one of them. I peered from behind a tree and observed a man with a machine that amplified his voice lead the group as they marched about.

"No more group homes! No more tax cheats!" the man shouted.

The group walked around in a circle, repeating the

man's chant. Eventually a van showed up and a camera crew began filming them.

At least they weren't hunting *me* with their cameras.

A young, dark-skinned female looked into the camera and described what was going on. "These protestors say that Deception Falls is already saturated with group homes for the disabled and that everyone's property taxes will go up if this home, which is empty right now, is taken off the tax rolls."

"You got that right!" shouted the man with the voice machine.

"What's your name, sir?" the television woman asked.

The shifty-eyed, dark-haired man smiled into the camera. "My name's Vincent Zambelli."

"How long have you lived in Deception Falls?"

"Just a few years. I retired from law enforcement on the East Coast and came out here on my pension. This is the kind of government bullying that made me move. Now it's happening here."

"What about those who say that the disabled need a place to live."

"There are other places for them to live. Let some other town down the coast foot the bill."

The television crew packed their equipment and left; the people dispersed. No one noticed me, of course. Then the tall, steel-jawed sheriff pulled up in his police car. The motto *Compassion and Excellence* was scrolled on the door of the vehicle. I knew this stern-looking man pretty well: he watched Deception Falls almost as much as I did. His name was Jack LaHood.

He rolled down the car window. "I thought you were gonna get a permit for your protest, Vincent."

"You can call me Vinny, Sheriff."

LaHood glared at him. "I'm callin' you Vincent. And don't give me any of that New Jersey buddy cop crap.

We got laws here too ya' know. Even retired law enforcement has to respect them."

"Okay, LaHood. I hear you, but the mayor's caved in way too easy on this one. He's kissed the state's ass on this group home."

"You're here for two years and you're an expert on Washington State politics. I'm hearin' that you're gonna take a run at the mayor? You think that people here are gonna vote you in over Jimmy Wallace?"

Zambelli smirked. "You never know."

"This is my town. I know it like the back of my hand. We aint votin' for some thug from New Jersey. Next time, get a permit or I'll bust you and cart you off to my jail for a night. It's my town, Vincent." LaHood rolled up his window and drove away.

So, Vincent Zambelli just moved here and he's holding a protest to keep other people – people weaker than himself - out. People with power, shoving weaker people around, shutting weaker people out. This is what happened to the native people when the first people from the East came with their guns and machines. It's one of the reasons why we stay in the shadows.

And this Sheriff becomes threatening, the minute he doesn't like someone.

I still can't figure out how humans have managed to dominate the land when they possess such mindlessness. And yet they have. Shattuck the Gray insists that they've constructed vast cities in the lands further away from here. They must have built them on the bones and the land of those hunted down and slaughtered.

I spent a lot of time listening to the bearded rabbi who lectured his people on Saturdays and the young priest who lectured his on Sundays. I don't know what the difference was between the Saturday people and the Sunday people. They looked pretty much the same to me. They use different symbols but say similar things.

Be kind to each other. Respect each other. Take care of the weak.

Zambelli hears this in Sunday service and shows up the next day to protest against the weak. Then the Sherriff - with a slogan on his car door about compassion - shows up and threatens to arrest him.

Despite the humans, Deception Falls was quiet most nights. But the more I watched and listened, the more I learned. There were people who plotted to screw their business partners and their customers. There were men who lied to their wives; some even beat their women while their children watched. And there were people who drank too much alcohol and used other kinds of drugs.

Biker gangs cruised through the town, mostly on weekends. One night I saw a bunch of them get into a brawl in front of Tina's Coffee Shop.

One of the bikers, a hairy, three-hundred pounder, wore a leather jacket with *Big Foot, Black Forest Kings* written boldly across the back. He slammed another over-sized man from a rival gang against a telephone pole and put a knife to his throat.

"You tell that punk, Billy Bear, that D-Falls is our town!"

The man was bleeding hard from his head. "Why don't you tell him yourself, Big Foot?"

"I'm gonna cut your balls off and stuff them in your mouth, Paco."

"Piss-off, you fat slug!"

Sheriff LaHood and some deputies arrived before more violence could occur and took some of the bikers away in handcuffs. The one called Big Foot spat at LaHood and received a club strike across the face before LaHood slammed him into his car door right above the *Compassion and Excellence* motto.

The one called Big Foot was indeed a nasty thug. His

breath reeked of beer and his black eyes seethed with violent potential. I wanted to rip his leather jacket off and strangle him with it.

The next morning, LaHood and his deputies took the handcuffed bikers across the street toward the town court. "I'm asking Judge Holland for max bail on you, Big Foot," LaHood said as he and his deputies walked the men into the old wooden court house.

I hid under a foot bridge that went over the stream in the parking lot behind the building. Though it offered good concealment, it was hard to hear what was going on inside the court house from so far away, so I followed the creek to the rear of the building. Using bushes for cover, I peered through the window. A female stood next to LaHood. She had a stack of paper on her desk. A male stood next to Big Foot, who looked as if he'd been beaten up. I couldn't get a look at the grey-haired Judge Holland because her back was to me.

The female spoke. "The people charge the defendant with assault, riot first degree and disorderly conduct, Your Honor."

"How does your client plead?" Holland asked.

It got quiet for a while, then, "Not guilty, Your Honor."

"Crock of shit." I heard LaHood whisper.

"Watch your tone, Sheriff," Holland said. "Be aware that the court has good hearing."

The woman looked at LaHood and shook her head. "We request twenty-five thousand dollars bail, Your Honor."

"That's unreasonable, Judge," the man standing next to Big Foot said. "My client's record is not that bad. No felony convictions. Always made his court appearances."

The woman turned toward Big Foot's advocate. "The offender has a significant arrest record, has terrorized the community, and may be involved in other offenses."

"He's a gangster thug," LaHood said loudly.

"He's a member of a biker club, Your Honor," the male said. "And he has a right to assemble with like-minded people."

"Court sets bail at ten thousand dollars."

The conversation ended and Judge Holland went on to other cases. I went back to hiding under the bridge and took a nap. A little while later, I woke to see Big Foot walking toward the stream talking to another gang member.

"LaHood can kiss my ass," Big Foot said. "Thanks for posting the bail money."

"No problem. We need to get Billy Bear and his bull-shit gang out of D-Falls or someday we might not have bail money sitting around."

"This punk-ass town is ours, Lenny - our little money maker. We control the flow of *H* and we were here first. Speaking of flow, I gotta take a wicked piss."

Big Foot walked to the side of the bridge and pissed into the stream. This stream flows into the Skokum River, from which my people drink.

I wanted to tear his spleen out.

I stayed under the bridge until nightfall and then walked back into the woods. That evening, I noticed activity in the Mount Olympus Park Ranger's cabin. The old place had been empty for a few months; recently, a female and her young son had moved in. Rangers had been allowed to live in it for some reason. I'd seen them come and go over the years.

The boy was odd. I could hear him humming and clapping his hands. I had the strange feeling that he was calling to me. I crept up closer to the cabin and peered into the boy's room. He was sitting on his bed, rocking back and forth, flapping his hands in an excited way. He was watching the same scene on a video over and over again. From the words in the music, I gathered that the film was called *Beauty and The Beast*.

His mother came into his room, still in her Ranger uniform. "Christopher, let's watch a different tape."

He protested, but she changed the tape anyway - something about a hairy blue monster that ate cookies. The kid started smacking his head with his palms and then biting his hands. "All right! All right. I'll put it back in. But promise to watch it all the way through. Stop repeating the same scenes."

Christopher nodded and went back to rocking back and forth and flapping his hands.

It was odd, but I sensed that the beast in the first movie comforted him. He began flapping his hands every time the creature appeared in the film. Eventually, the film ended and Christopher fell asleep.

This family was different from the other human families. There was something haunting about the blue-eyed boy that intrigued me.

I watched the cabin all night. The child woke up twice and shouted loudly, waking his mother. On both occasions, she came into his room and sang to him until he fell asleep, gently caressing his hair.

And that was the odd thing. Although I was outside, I could see them in his room and felt as though I were in there with them.

I could see his eyes looking out into the night, as though there was a message that he was sending. But to whom?

The next morning, a bus marked *Cascadia Special Educational Services* picked the child up for school. The mother, looking exhausted, got into her Park Ranger vehicle and left for work. I felt a pall of sadness about the woman. She had dark hair and deep blue eyes that seemed full of worry. She was beautiful, for a human female.

What was wrong with her son? Why was he so different from everyone else I had watched?

Chapter Four

YOU LEARN A lot about people from what they throw away, so I regularly visited the town dump. The place was a fragrant bouquet of foul odors. But one scent was unmistakable - the scent of death. I climbed a pile and tossed some trash aside. There was an old refrigerator partially buried in the mound. I opened it. Inside was a dead man. From the smell, he'd been there for about a week.

So much for refrigeration.

Even in his purple, bloated state, I could see that he was one of the bikers: tattoos and a beard. He was wearing a jacket with the words, Paco Jimenez - Pacific Coast Warriors written across the back. This was the brute that Big Foot Nolan threatened to castrate. I wondered if Nolan had carried out that threat, but it didn't much matter because the cause of death was obviously lead poisoning—old Paco took one right between the eyes.

The compassionate Sherriff LaHood needed to work a little harder. Clearly, he wasn't having much success dealing with the local gang problem. Some biker was stuffed in a refrigerator and he didn't even know about it. I decided that he should.

I dragged Paco out of the dump.

Later that evening, I watched LaHood from the woods as he walked out of Tina's Coffee Shop into the parking lot holding a donut. He spit his coffee out when he came upon Paco's carcass, mouth agape, lying on the roof of his police car.

"What the hell!?"

Within a few minutes, every police car from the town, sirens wailing, poured into the parking lot.

"Don't touch nuthin'," LaHood barked to his deputies. "I want the area taped off and everythin' photographed."

"Oh wow!" said one of his deputies approaching the vehicle. "How'd he get up there?"

LaHood glared at the deputy. "Soon as I figure that out, I'll let ya know."

"This is a big dude, Sheriff. Couldn't have been easy to stick him up there."

"Obviously. I pulled in ten minutes ago. Got a donut. Shot the shit with Tina for a minute and strolled out here to this nightmare."

"You didn't hear anything?"

"Nuthin'."

"Looks like he's been dead a while."

LaHood looked at the man incredulously. "No shit, he's been dead a while. You don't turn purple and stink to high hell unless you been dead a while. Gimme' your flash light."

The deputy retrieved one from the trunk of his car. LaHood leaned over the body and illuminated Paco's face. "This is one of the bikers, Raymond. In fact, you arrested this one for possessing drugs a few weeks ago."

The deputy leaned in. "You're right, Sheriff...Oh God!" the deputy bolted a few steps away and vomited behind his car. "That's Paco Jimenez. One of the Pacific Coast Warriors."

LaHood continued to shine the light on the body and roof of his cruiser. "Well someone gave old Paco a third eye socket."

"How can you handle the stench? You aren't nauseous?"

"Been at every autopsy in the town for the past decade. You get used to it. Only see this one wound. Looks like it was an execution." He turned to the deputies. "Is Maxine on the way?"

"Medical Examiner's finishing dinner. Says she'll be right over," another officer responded.

LaHood nodded. "She might wanna eat light. All right, I want everything photographed where it sits. Nobody touches anything."

"What about your car, sir?" Raymond asked nervously.

LaHood shook his head. "It stays here with old Paco until we get a look at everything in the daylight. It's part of this crime scene." He walked over to Raymond's car. "You'll have to drive me home later." He motioned his officers to gather around him. "I want every biker in this town brought in and questioned. We're findin' out who killed this man and we're sending their asses to the gallows. Sons-of-bitches ruined my cruiser!"

The town was now a powder keg, ready to go off because of the feuding biker gangs. The sheriff's headquarters were the focus of a lot of tension. I kept a close eye on the building and listened to every conversation that I could. You learn a lot about humans by the other humans they arrest.

LaHood's men brought in biker after biker and interrogated each one.

The groups terrorizing each other—and Deception Falls—were the Pacific Coast Warriors, led by Billy-Bear Rollins, and the Black Forest Kings, led by the vile Bobby

"Big Foot" Nolan. Both gangs wanted exclusive sales rights for "H", which I learned was something called heroin. Both gangs claimed the town as their turf and that only made me hate them more.

I know exactly whose turf this is.

"Word is that Rollins' boys are takin' your business, Big Foot," LaHood said.

"I make an honest living repairing motor cycles, Sherriff," Nolan responded.

"You haven't had an honest day in your miserable life, Nolan."

"I would really like advice of counsel if you're gonna 'cuse me of any criminal behavior. I'm just a regular citizen."

"Regular citizen, my ass!"

Then I heard punches landing and what seemed to be a body slammed onto the floor. "Sheriff! Take it easy!" shouted another deputy.

From the sound of it, Nolan wasn't having a pleasant visit to police headquarters. So be it. Nolan pissed me off when he urinated in my water supply that day after the court proceedings. Judge Holland should have kept him in jail. This three-hundred-pound, tattooed abomination of evolution named himself after my gang. This goon spent his evenings waddling around The Biker's Hole Bar and Grill, spilling beer and bragging how proud he was of his "colors"

The next day, LaHood brought in the smug, muscular, black-shirted Billy Bear Rollins. It was his turn to experience LaHood's unique interrogation style.

"You gonna let your man's death go unsolved, Rollins?" LaHood asked.

"I'm not a detective. You figure out who killed him. You're the law. You take care of it."

"Don't bullshit me, punk. We both know that you're gonna take revenge. It's what you gangsters do. Unless you're figurin' we'd carry the ball for you. Is that why you dumped Paco's body on my cruiser?"

"Piss off, Sheriff. I want an attorney."

"Answer my question!"

"Ghhhack! I can't answer you...you're choking me, you pig!"

"I oughta stick my gun in your mouth and let you choke on a bullet!"

"Sheriff!" Once again, I heard the sound of other deputies running into the room to stop the beating.

"We would never desecrate the body of a dead brother that way!" Rollins shouted.

"Dead brother, my ass! I'm a Marine," LaHood yelled. "I know what it is to lose a brother in battle. You're just a bunch of drug dealers."

"Paco died with his colors on!" Rollins countered.

LaHood was getting pressure from Mayor Jimmy Wallace, who was calling incessantly about the mayhem the biker gangs were causing in town. One night, the round-faced Wallace visited LaHood.

"I don't know what to make of it, Jimmy. Neither gang benefitted from having Paco's corpse dumped on my cruiser."

"This is supposed to be a sleepy little town - not a war zone."

"I was in the Gulf War. The tension feels close to that. Zambelli came in this afternoon and got a permit to protest in front of the group home again. When do those people move in, Jimmy?"

"Next week."

"That ginzo is gunning for your job."

"These people need a place to live, Jack. His taxes may go up five dollars and these poor people are in wheel chairs. They're not a threat to anyone," the mayor said evenly.

"It's your classic 'not in my back yard' crap. This guy

is turning everyone in the town against each other. And now I have these leather-jacketed bastards scaring citizens out of their minds."

"Jack, you heard about Councilman Lightfoot's son?"

"Yeah," LaHood said. "It was fentanyl laced heroin. Another one."

"The kid was in law school. Had everything going for him. Gets his appendix out last year and gets hooked on the pain killers they gave him."

"Just like my son," LaHood whispered bitterly. "Pharma sets them up, then gangsters like Nolan and Rollins swoop in, make their money and finish them off."

"I'm sorry, Jack. I should have come over quicker to tell you. I knew this would be more salt in the wound. I didn't want you to learn about it from people around town."

"It's my job, Jimmy, to know what's bein' said 'round the town."

The Mayor paused, "Stuffing a dead biker on top of your car - it doesn't make sense."

"We still can't figure how someone, heck, even a group of people, could dump somethin' that heavy on my car, un-noticed. Coroner said she'd never seen nuthin' like it. Maxine said that Paco'd been dead for a week. And my car still stinks to high hell. Whoever did this is an absolute ghoul. It also might have started a gang war."

Chapter Five

THE NEXT NIGHT I turned my attention to the Biker's Hole Bar and Grill. Looming in the woods that surrounded the establishment, I peered into the bar to see what was going on.

I could have gone in and ordered a meal. The place was so noisy and the patrons so stupid that they likely wouldn't have noticed me. But I stayed by the window and observed the parade of idiots marching by. Both gangs were there that night and there was drunken, palpable tension. The Black Forest Kings played billiards on my side of the place and Billy Bear and the Pacific Coast Warriors shot pool on the other. Bobby Big Foot left his jacket on the chair under the window while he played pool and glared across the bar at Billy Bear.

Two rivals in the middle of the bar traded insults and glared at each other while screwing chalk onto the tips of their pool ques.

"Gentleman!" the bar tender shouted, "Just chill out and play pool."

This was my chance to exact revenge. When everyone turned toward the bar tender, I reached in and took

Bobby Big Foot's leather jacket off of the chair under the window. It was time to give Bobby Big Foot's colors the respect they deserved.

I urinated all over his jacket and placed it neatly back on his chair.

Be advised that my kind possess a level of expertise in marking territory that is the envy of the animal kingdom. When we mark, we mean it.

Drunk and stupid though he was, it didn't take Bobby long to notice that someone had *disrespected* his colors.

"Who pissed on my jacket?" he bellowed.

Everybody froze.

"Who pissed on my colors?" He drew a handgun from the small of his back and pointed it at Billy-Bear. "Answer me, Rollins!"

Now this was getting interesting.

"I don't what you're talking about, you fat piece of..."

The bar tender pulled out a shotgun. "Put the gun away, Bobby. I don't need this crap. Town's gonna close me down if we have any more problems."

"I don't care about this town!"

"Sheriff's coming down on me, Bobby. I don't need to be dragged in and hit with more fines. LaHood's gonna close my bar."

"Screw your filthy bar, Kenny," Big Foot shouted. "Someone peed all over my jacket. Smells like a dead water buffalo."

"You already smelled like a dead water buffalo," Billy-Bear smirked.

Oh, this is going to be glorious!

Another leather-jacketed Pacific Coast Warrior pulled his gun and pointed it at Bobby. "What's it gonna be, Big Foot?"

Do we have to call this grunting slob, *Big Foot* all the time?

Bobby Big Foot was red with rage. "Who pissed on my colors?"

"I'll pay for the dry cleaning, for Chris' sakes," the bar tender shouted.

"That's not the point, Kenny. I want someone's balls in a basket."

"Then you'll have just have to shoot me," Billy Bear said smiling smugly. "You fat piece of shit."

I have to hand it to Billy Bear. He died with his colors on.

Bobby Big Foot blasted away and the whole place erupted in gun fire. As bullets blew through the walls, I had to seek cover behind a tree. I could hear round after round going off as bikers and their girls screamed in agony and terror. Gang members poured out the front door, guns drawn, raining bullets into the parking lot. Some bikers tore away on their motor cycles, still shooting. One was hit as he drove away and crashed into a tree somewhere down the road. A woman tried to climb out the window where I had been standing earlier. She pushed her head through and saw me watching her from behind the tree.

"What the hell are you?" she screamed, astonished.

Then a round blew off the back of her head. She ended up hanging half out the window, eyes still open in death.

There was more shouting, gun fire, and cries of agony. Then silence.

I waited to make sure the shooting stopped then peered in over the body of the dead girl. Victims were lying on the blood-splattered floor. Some were moaning, still clinging to life. There was blood and shattered glass covering the bar. I guessed that Kenny's problems with Sherriff LaHood would no longer worry him - his arm hung lifelessly over the half-door leading to the area behind the bar. Billy Bear lay dead on what was an otherwise lovely green billiard table, staring at the ceiling fan.

Bobby Big Foot was on his side, bleeding from multiple wounds to his chest, choking on his own blood. He saw me looking at him and pointed at me, amazed. He moved for his gun but I reached in and swatted it away. Then I took his jacket. He grabbed a sleeve and wouldn't let go of it.

"You pissed in my water," I said.

He coughed up blood. "You...*you* pissed on my colors!"

"It was I, Sasquatch."

"*You* did this?" He struggled to hold the jacket. "My colors...a *monster* is taking my colors."

"You killed people over this rag. And you call *me* a monster?" I snatched the jacket from his trembling hands. A moment later, he was dead.

The impact of my intervention with the gangs provided me with a profound insight: I didn't have to kill humans. All I had to do was create the opportunity for them to kill each other and they would do what humans do.

It was the happiest I'd felt in weeks. I ran into the woods holding Big Foot's jacket like a trophy and climbed to the top of a steep hill. *"YEEWAAAAH!"* I bellowed down into the valley, waving the jacket in the air.

"What is going on with you?" It was Shattuck the Gray, messaging me. "You're scaring me. Did you do something to the humans?"

"Not exactly...but I did see them killing each other with abandon in the town."

"It is what they do. You need to stay away from the town, away from the humans."

"They killed my son."

"This blood lust can take you down a dark path. You don't know of our past with them."

"We should kill them all."

"Redirect your energies."

"How?"

"I have consulted with the others. We will send you some new women from other domains. That should occupy you."

"*WAAAAHAH!*" I screamed in triumph.

Later that night, I threw Bobby Big Foot's jacket into the dump.

Chapter Six

"THE MALES FROM my father's domain can't get Brown Bears to catch salmon for them," the pretty young female from the North woods said.

This new one had to come to me, just as Shattuck had promised. She was worth the wait. We held each other, watching Grizzlies catch and eat salmon swimming against the current to reach their spawning grounds. The bears waded through the icy waters of a roaring rapid at the bottom of a steep canyon. It was an epic setting for an epic romance.

"This is how I run things here," I smiled. "Look, here comes another one." A large male delivered a wriggling, juicy salmon and gave it to me. "This one's full of roe," I handed her the fish.

"I could get used to this." Her eyes glowed with youthful sincerity. "You will be gentle with me, I hope."

I smiled knowingly.

The bear-catching-salmon technique never fails to impress the ladies. My father instructed me years ago on how to work with the other apex predators in my lands. Thus, Brown Bears, Cougars, and all the rest do our bidding and won't hunt our young. We're not exclusively carnivorous so we can supplement our diet with plants, craw fish, mussels and small animals. Our lands are abundant with life, yet when I make a kill, it is shared with the other predators. It's a good policy on multiple levels – snoopy humans can't differentiate our techniques from the work of other hunters – and I keep the competitors happy.

Keep techniques secret but always share meat.

A while later we snuggled under a pine tree, enjoying the afterglow. Then the mood changed. My head was flooded with urgent mind messages from others. *"A skinny human woman is watching you and the new one from a bluff overlooking the river. She has a small machine with three legs."*

I knew what *a small machine with legs* meant from dealing with Hasselbeck. We were being filmed!

I slowly moved a branch so I could see what the others were seeing. There she was. "Stay here, little one, I won't be long."

Through the trees I went, silent, purple rage burning in my eyes. I scaled the cliff then descended to the bluff. The thin woman didn't notice me until I landed with a resounding *thump*.

"Give me the camera," I roared.

"Ahh! Ahh!" She scrambled to her feet, grabbed her equipment, and moved to the edge of the bluff in panic. Snack bars and other provisions spilled out onto the grass from her opened backpack. I was afraid she'd jump. And there was no way this boney, granola-chewing nit-wit would survive a seventy-foot drop onto a rock-filled, raging river full of salmon-hunting bears.

"Shut up," I said with mounting rage.

"Help! Help!"

"Shut your mouth or I'll smash your skull against the rocks!"

"Oh my God! Are you gonna *kill* me?" she managed, trembling with terror.

"If you're lucky, I'll just erase the memory of this encounter from your mind. You'll wander through the woods, disoriented for a few days. Happens to people all the time. You will blame it on hypothermia."

"My God! you can *talk* and *reason,* too."

"What do you mean by *too*?"

"Uh, I just mean, that, um along with your other... impressive, sophisticated behaviors," she flattered, trying to regain control.

I moved in closer, enraged. "Lady, give me the camera. You had no right to film my *impressive, sophisticated* behaviors."

"I'm sorry. I had no intention of filming *you*. I was filming the bears - a nature program for public television."

"So, this was an accident? Very well. That gives me reason to reconsider killing you, which normally, I would," I said with the sarcasm she deserved for thinking me stupid.

"Hey, hey. You're not really thinking about killing me, right?" she said holding her hands out as though to caution me. "This film could help you. It will help get habitat protection laws passed, environmental preservation acts. I'm a Progressive, you know."

"You're insane."

"This film is incredibly valuable. The public has a right to see it."

"No they don't! Do they have a right to see *you* mating?"

"Some celebrities have made this kind of thing work for them," she reasoned.

I gritted my teeth, wanting to kill her, just get rid of her, but I answered. "Critics will just say that it was a hoax, two people in monkey costumes."

She smiled sheepishly. "Nobody could design a costume to do what you just did, fella." She was feeling confident.

"You're really pissing me off!"

She began to shake again. "The government will step in to protect your species. I can help you."

"Lady, the government said that they'd help the native people around here. How did that work out? Give me the camera." I moved in closer.

"I'm a Liberal and a Democrat." She inched closer to the edge of the cliff. "I've briefed the Governor on the brown bears. Got a new state program that lowered the bow hunting quota. I can help you too."

"I don't need your help. We don't need a state program. Give it to me and go protect some other species." I grabbed the camera. To my amazement, she refused to let go. "Let go of the camera!"

"No!"

"Give it to me!"

"I can protect you."

"You can't protect anything. Give it to me!"

"I'm a Liberal!"

I yanked it from her and she fell back, tumbling over the edge into the chasm.

"Now you're just meat." When I looked down, I could see her body slamming into the rocks in the white water, face down. A few minutes later, the bears had her.

I felt badly about the death of the Liberal. She was sincere and idealistic, in a stupid sort of way.

And I was worried. Humans were ending up dead when they encountered me, even when I didn't intend to kill them. Had my desire for revenge brought bad magic?

I decided that I had to do something that I hadn't done in years. It was time to visit the Shaman of the local native people. Maybe he could advise me about what to do.

I ate the Liberal's granola bars and smashed the camera.

Chapter Seven

I SPENT THE FIRST part of the next evening sitting in the rain, watching Christopher rocking back and forth in his room in front of the television. His mother had a man over for dinner, a red-haired, muscular fellow. I sensed that Christopher didn't feel comfortable with him.

What kind of deer scat was going on between my ears? Why did I think I could sense what this damaged child felt? The time I was spending watching Christopher was interfering with my surveillance of the town's miserable residents.

I needed to get back to my work with the towns people. Facilitating their self-destructive tendencies took a lot of energy. Since the biker gangs had annihilated each other, I needed a new focus. While that intervention was wildly successful, I've always believed that one shouldn't rest on the glories of past hunts. I needed to get back in the game.

But first, I had to visit Salli Tani'm, the Shaman of the Red Cedar Tribe. The whites call him Two-Moons.

I arrived at the tribal long house after midnight in a torrent of rain. The Shaman lived next to it in a small cabin behind the totem that had my image carved into it. There was a whale at the bottom, me in the middle, and a scary, giant Thunderbird with bared teeth capping the top.

The Thunderbird is to be respected. When he appears, it is a sign that things are going to change. As I always did, I paused to acknowledge him.

Many in the tribe felt that old, half-blind Two-Moons was crazy and eccentric. He was old and though his vision was failing, he wasn't crazy. Yes, he was eccentric. But Shaman are always eccentric. That's why they're Shaman.

I looked through the window and saw him sitting in his rocking chair in front of the fire place. A blanket with the image of an enormous red bird was draped over him. His long grey hair hung over the back of the rocker. I quietly opened the door and slid into the cabin.

"If you intend to harm me, I'm gonna shoot. I can still see," he said turning around with alarm.

"I intend you no harm, old one. If I did, you'd be dead already."

"My hairy brother, you've returned! I was worried that you'd gone."

"I am as I ever was."

"Touch my hand," he said. "I need to feel your flesh." I put my hand on his. His eyes glistened with tears. "I am so happy. The spirit of the dark woods still roams among us. I prayed that you would come again. I have something for you." He rose from the chair; he was old and feeble, but suddenly full of energy. He opened his refrigerator and rummaged. "I have some deer meat for you. Look." He handed me the meat to see.

"I brought you some salmon, old one." I handed him the fish wrapped in newspaper from the recycling bin at the Ranger cabin. An offering of salmon is always welcome among the Chinook.

Two-Moons smiled as he unwrapped the fish. "May I cook the salmon later?"

"Whenever you want. This deer meat is fresh, let's enjoy it now."

He opened a drawer by the sink. "My teenage nephew brought it today," Two-Moons said, taking the meat back and putting a long fork through it. "I was surprised. I was beginning to feel that the kid was useless." He showed a photograph of him. "I was calling him *useless as whale shit*, but I was wrong." He cooked the meat over his fire.

"How old is he?

"He's sixteen. You know how teenagers are." He looked into the flames as though he were looking at something far away. Then he turned to me. "I see now. You lost a teen-age child." He looked at me with compassion. "That's why you've come." He stared into the fire with greater intensity. "It was a bearded hunter. He would've killed you, too, but you got him first. I had a dream about this the night of the mourning cries. I am so sorry, my brother."

"You still live in the *real* world, old one."

He nodded. "I have to. This modern world isn't real. You should see what's on TV these days. The Europeans call them *reality shows*. They have one program about people looking for you." Two-Moons shook his head. "How can reality also be a show? The modern world isn't real. It's an illusion."

"So much of life is an illusion. Two-Moons, I seek your advice. I fear that I can't control my desire for revenge. I've done some strange things lately. Violent things."

He pointed at the TV. "No one could be as strange as these people. Revenge against them is useless, my brother. They eventually kill themselves."

"And everyone else. I fear that I've unleashed bad magic."

"You didn't. They did."

He held the meat over the flame. "Right now, they are planning to extend an oil pipeline into our lands. Some in the tribe say we shouldn't fight this. They say it may bring jobs. But these corporate invaders want to run this thing over our ancestor's burial site, our sacred ground." He turned to me and our eyes met. "This is desecration."

"I would kill anyone who threatened our sacred places."

The old man nodded. "I've taken an oath to protect this land. I will stand against the oil company and the government. I'll die if I have to."

"So, you, too, are assigned to protect the spirits of your ancestors."

"When we allow those with power and money to inflict their will upon those who have less, we move away from who we really are." He looked at the meat. "I am organizing a protest against the pipeline."

"Do you have any advice for me?"

"What do your elders say?"

"They keep sending me new women."

Two-Moons smiled. "Those are my kind of elders, brother."

"I cannot defy them."

"Our tribal elders would merely write a letter to the federal government." He put his hand on my shoulder. "Good thing the salmon are running, eh?" He handed me some deer meat. "Finish the meat, my brother. You need energy for your women." He walked over to a book case and took down a small bowl. "Is this bowl brown or red?" he asked, squinting.

"Red," I answered.

"Good. Stand away from the fireplace for a minute. If a spark lands on me, deal with it. Don't let me catch fire. Burning up is a horrible way to die." He cleared his throat and nodded. "I'm going to go into a trance." He threw powder from the red bowl into the fireplace. The fire spewed sparks and the room filled with smoke. He kept waving the smoke toward himself.

Two-Moons didn't catch fire. If he had, I wouldn't have been able to help him. I was completely stoned by the drug-infused smoke within moments. A massive, wild-man in an altered state of consciousness is not a good thing to have stumbling around your living room. I got dizzy, crashed into his rocking chair, and passed out.

I woke a while later to see Two-Moons lying in front of the fire place under his blanket. I reached over and shook him. "Old man." He didn't respond. Had I killed another human?

Then his eyes opened. Slowly he rose to his feet. "Looks like you owe me a new rocking chair," he smiled. "That was an interesting journey last night, huh?"

"What happened?"

"Don't worry. Just drink a lot of water today. We took a trip."

"Where did we go?"

"We traveled through consciousness. I know for sure that you have to keep an eye on an unusual kid in the Ranger cabin."

"Why?"

"I don't know why. But there is some heavy magic surrounding that kid."

Chapter Eight

I LOOKED IN ON Police Headquarters shortly after sundown. From the hill in the rear of the building, I could see through the windows of the conference room. There was some celebrating going on. From what I could see posted on the white board, the other policemen were throwing Sheriff LaHood a party for "Twenty-five Years on the Job." Mayor Wallace read a statement about LaHood's commitment to the town and all the fine work he'd done for the residents. Everyone applauded.

I guess we're going to gloss over that little massacre at the Biker's Hole Bar and Grill.

LaHood was presented with some gifts: a fruit basket, a paper called *a gift certificate* and a rocking chair. Everyone had a good laugh over the rocker.

A certain Shaman needed one of those.

It was time for a creative diversion. I walked through the woods to the parking lot where the police vehicles were parked and looked the place over. Police cars filled the lot. There was some barbed wire atop a fence—hardly an obstacle for me. No security cameras. That made sense. Even a human wouldn't be stupid enough to steal a car from the police station. Stealing wasn't my plan. I just needed to have one of the cars make that annoying wailing sound they make. I knew that police come running to the scene when the cars make that maddening noise.

I moved in and quietly took the fence down. LaHood's car seemed to have its own special spot on a slight rise; a sign there read *Sheriff*. I punched in the window on the driver's side and tried to figure out how to open the door. I couldn't, so I just tore it off. The inside of the vehicle was a maze of buttons and switches and equipment. I couldn't tell what did what. The wheel used for steering was in the way so I ripped that out and threw it on the ground.

All the switches and buttons - what do they do? I leaned in with mounting frustration and tried to figure the machine out. I started pressing all the buttons which turned on lights and set off the noise maker as well. I also did something wrong: the car started rolling down the rise toward the other parked cars.

I picked up the steering wheel and ran back into the woods. The Sheriff's vehicle slammed into the other parked police cars in a series of loud crashes triggering more alarms. It stopped only after it pounded into the rear entrance of the building, shattering the glass doors in a violent crash.

Agitated policeman poured into the parking lot.

"My new cruiser!" LaHood shouted as he got to the scene.

I threw the steering wheel through the conference room window and grabbed the rocking chair.

A little while later, I checked in on Christopher. As usual, he was moaning and flapping his hands. He was watching some TV show about a crew of people traveling around the stars. I guess it made some sense. I've seen the noisy sky machines. I figured that they were another variety of human transport.

Humans are always going somewhere. This is why they never stop to look at what's around them.

The leader of the space ship is a bit full of himself and enjoys looking at the females who serve him. I find it intriguing that he relies on a fellow who is clearly another type of human who has pointed ears. I like this pointy-eared variant. He seems to realize that humans are crazy, but he endures them. Maybe that's what I have to do.

Christopher's mother came in and sang to him sweetly. From listening to her phone calls, I've learned that her name is Marianna. She has dark hair and fierce blue eyes, like Christopher's. She is petite and looks funny with a gun on her hip in that ridiculous green uniform the Parks Service makes her wear.

This is another way that humans are bat-shit crazy beyond my comprehension. They think that they transform themselves by changing clothes. That kind of work involves more than a costume change.

Christopher falls asleep. I hunker down for a nap, too, and fall into a deep sleep.

I see stars flying by. I am flying through space. *Seek truth with peace in your heart and you will see the creator all around you.*

I wake with a start. Who said that? It wasn't a mind message from anyone I knew.

I looked at the stars and realized from their positions in the sky that I'd been sleeping for a while. Christopher was asleep. Marianna and her boyfriend were together in her part of the cabin.

Time to move on.

I start getting messages from the others. Hasselbeck and the crew are back. I climbed to the top of a nearby mountain, and from a perch I learn that they are employing a new technique.

Hasselbeck installed some secret cameras on certain

trees to see if they could catch an image of me reaching up for some packages of fresh meat and bacon planted high in the branches. As if I wouldn't notice the cameras. As if I would be so easily provoked by the smell of their bacon.

Do Hasselbeck and his team really think that I'm that simple? I can have fresh meat whenever I want in my domain. I understand humans and their addiction to manipulating the natural world. But does this moron really believe he can capture me with a camera that flashes every time a Mule Deer wanders by? You humans are the simple ones watching fantasies on TV and hoping to find Big Foot.

The smell of the bacon was making me nuts, though. Good smoked bacon is hard to come by in these parts.

They wandered around the woods with night vision goggles after they installed the cameras and baits. In no time, they were howling and tree knocking as usual. They always believe that one of us will reply with our own tree-knock. I decided that this time, I would respond.

I came down from the mountain with an oak club. I moved behind the first tree on which they had installed a camera. The smell of bacon was intoxicating. I side-swiped the camera with a devastating swing. Take my word on this, when I swing oak at something, the some-thing is transformed—permanently. What was once a marvelous piece of technology was now a hunk of shat-tered plastic and metal dangling from the tree.

The bacon was mine.

"I heard a tree knock!" Hasselbeck rasped into his radio.

That's funny, Hasselbeck. What I heard was an expen-sive camera getting smashed into high tech garbage.

"Let's do some more knocks," he whispered into his radio. His minions dutifully obeyed.

And I responded by pounding more cameras into obliv-ion and eating more bacon. Now that's what tree knock-ing is all about.

Hasselbeck stood triumphant in front of the film crew. "We've just had an amazing night of Big Footing. We've never had so much tree knocking behavior in one night."

I've never eaten so much bacon.

"I think it's possible that all we might have heard tonight was other humans responding to our tree knocks," said team member Rachel to the camera man. "There's still no proof of Big Foot."

I like this skeptical woman. She thinks for herself and isn't afraid to stand up to Hasselbeck. One shouldn't just accept everything a leader says. Of course, she's completely wrong.

The next morning, Hasselbeck figured out what had really gone on.

"We just lost twenty-five thousand dollars in equipment!" he shouted toward Rachel. "How the hell are we gonna pay to replace this stuff?"

"Maybe Hank at the network can help out," she answered.

"The Natural World Network isn't going to reimburse us for this." He turned toward the camera man who had been filming their exchange. "Turn the camera off."

Rachel shook her head. "This supports what I said last night. People were doing the wood knocking. Those people vandalized our equipment."

"You should call the Park Rangers and file a report," the camera man said. "You'll need a police report for the insurance claim."

"I think that a Big Foot did this," Hasselbeck insisted.

"Joey, I know that last night was thrilling. Even I was amazed. It's not that I don't want to believe that these animals exist. But the facts lead me to conclude that we were screwed with, nothing more."

"Would they have taken the bacon?"

"Why not?" Rachel rolled her eyes. "They were screwing with us."

"I think it was a Squatch. Those cameras were pulverized."

"Come on, Joe. An animal couldn't do that."

"Rachel, when I encountered that Big Foot all those years ago in Northern California, I know what I saw. And what I saw was more than an animal. It was huge. It was intelligent."

"If these primates exist, I'm sure they are."

"You're not hearing me. What I saw was, well, transformative."

Chapter Nine

FROM THE DARKNESS on the edge of Deception Falls, all things become clear. In the weeks since the biker-gang massacre, the town's twisted residents have moved on. I hear in whispers what they will not speak aloud.

"They weren't from here."

"They were violent people. Nothing like us."

"They dressed like thugs."

"They did drugs."

"They were gangsters and they got what was coming to them."

Really? I'm sure that's what the woman who encountered me in the window of the bar thought just before a bullet ripped through her skull.

See Sasquatch and die.

The hypocrisy of the hairless ones does not fill one with hope for the future. The priest and rabbi try their best, I give them that. I listen to their sermons to the self-centered barbarians who walk through their doors. They try to get them to do right, but the religious ones are just pissing into the wind. Within a few hours of leaving, their faithful will be eating their fill from a rich dish of treachery and deceit.

I heard the rabbi tell a tale about two ancient brothers named Cain and Abel to a temple packed with the faithful. I could hear the story clearly and powerfully from a perch, hidden behind a stand of Sitka Pine. "Where is your brother?" the rabbi asked. "Am I my brother's keeper? Your brother's blood cries out to me from the ground.... You will be a restless wanderer on the earth."

Is the sermon about me and my kind or you and your kind? I don't know. The story leaves me angry. Am I Abel or Cain?

Once the sun goes down, the games begin. That's when they lie and cheat on their partners, turn on their loved ones, and commit their crimes. It is not just the outsiders who bring shame to the town.

I watch a man standing on a street corner in the darkness, just outside of the reach of an overhead lamp. A car approaches and the windows roll own. The man approaches the car, glances around nervously, takes some money, and then hands the person in the car a small package. The man retreats into an alley as I watch the car pull away.

Something evil is going on. People buy all sorts of crap but they don't usually do it like that.

The car leaves town and climbs up the hills on a road I know well. I wonder if they plan to go to the clearing in the woods where I often see cars at night. Young humans go there to mate. Maybe the forest stirs their blood as it does for my kind.

A few minutes later, the nervous white man is back on the dark corner. Another car rolls up and money and a package are exchanged. Something bad is being sold here. I wonder if the religious leaders know about this street corner enterprise. I wonder if Sheriff LaHood knows.

I stop by Christopher's cabin and I immediately sense tension in the air. A woman is lecturing Marianna in the kitchen.

"Christopher's behavior has to improve or we may have to send him to a different school," the woman says sternly.

"I'm trying the best I can," Marianna pleads. "I've tried everything. I don't how to stop him from wandering."

"Has he ever eloped from the cabin?"

"No. He seems really happy here. I think the woods are good for him."

"Well he keeps wandering out of the building into the woods behind school. He's becoming a real management problem."

What's so bad about going for a walk in the woods?

The woman sat down at the kitchen table. "Sheriff LaHood says he can't keep deploying officers to the campus. It's a resource issue."

This Sheriff needs to do a better job securing his town. Instead of moaning about Christopher and sending people over to lecture his mother, LaHood should look at what's going on around him.

Marianna sobbed. "We just moved here. Please give him more time to adjust."

"This can't keep happening."

"Please, I love my son. He is so gentle but he can't tell anyone what he's feeling."

The woman takes off her glasses and places them on the table. "I know that he's non-verbal."

"He wouldn't hurt a fly. I've moved all around the state to find a situation that is safe for him. This is our last chance."

The woman offers some tissues to Marianna. "All right, we'll try a different reward program in the classroom. The teacher is a hopeful person. I shouldn't tell you this, but the teacher told LaHood to chill out." The woman put some papers in a folder on the table. "The Sheriff said that it's a good thing that you wear a badge and a uniform. We'll keep trying."

A while later, I see Marianna holding Christopher and crying while he watches TV on his bed.

With all that is wrong in Deception Falls, the town fathers have sent an agent to lecture this mother struggling with her unusual son. This family is just holding on. They're living in a run-down cabin on the edge of the woods, not even in the town itself. And still they turn on them because they're different.

You think that I should lead my kind out of the forest and interact with your race? You, who cannot manage to care for each other or show any degree of compassion. We should risk our futures on you?

I fall asleep under a pine tree and dream about the cars climbing the mountain road into the woods. Where are they going? I see that man in the alley, emerging from shadows, then returning to them. "Your brother's blood cries out to me from the ground...You will be a restless wanderer on the earth."

Images and faces in the shadows and light. Shadows and light...

"Are we Cain?" I ask Shattuck.

He answers with silence.

Shadows and light...shadows and light...

"Love all as your mother loved you."

"Even those who hate and hunt me?"

"Especially those. Blessed are the hunted, for they shall taste true freedom."

My eyes open. I can't tell who is sending me these messages and it is driving me crazy. Am I losing my mind?

A car pulls up in front of the cabin. It is Marianna's boyfriend. I can tell by the way he's walking that he's been drinking.

"Let's go out for some drinks, Darling. I love your eyes."

Marianna starts the coffee pot. "You've had enough. You need to lie down."

He kisses her. "C'mon, baby. You're so pretty. Let's have some fun."

"You're drunk already and I can't leave my son." She gently pushes him on to the couch. "You'll just have to stay."

I move through the woods and sense the presence of Hasselbeck. Going tree to tree, to conceal my approach, I move closer to a small tent that has a small camera pointed into it. Hasselbeck is talking to the camera.

"I'm here tonight taking a new approach. I'm going solo to see if I can attract some attention from the local Big Foot population."

I guess that Hasselbeck thinks that we in the local Big Foot population will just drop by for a snack and chat about the salmon run.

He adjusts the camera lens. "It's really quiet out here. This is a part of Big Footing that I love - being in the woods at night."

Love the woods, do you? I liked it here too - and then *you* showed up with your minions and camera crews. Who is watching this stuff? This must be the "reality show" that Two-Moons spoke of.

A light rain begins to fall. I hear the rain drops sizzling on the rocks around his camp fire. Hasselbeck begins packing his gear. "Time to turn in for the night. Rain's coming in." He turns the camera off and brings his equipment into the tent. Within a few minutes, the lights in the tent are out.

The rain is now heavier and the rocks in the fire pit spit steam. Smoke is rising into the rainy mist as the fire dies.

Emerging from the stand of trees, I stand over the tent, listening to Hasselbeck snoring. I draw a deep breath in, then..."*WAAHOOO!*"

My roar blows Hasselbeck out of his sleep – and his sleeping bag. "Oh! Oh!" I can see his shadow as he scrambles around the tent, frenetically searching for equipment. I disappear into the smoke and mist as though I never was.

Heading to a favorite cave for some sheltered sleep, I pass that opening in the forest where the couples park their cars. Sure enough, one of the cars involved in the exchange with the shadowy man on the street corner is there. I move slowly toward it and make out two figures in the car on opposite sides of the front seat. They are not moving. I rub the rain off the window and peer in. The male is slumped over the wheel, eyes open and lifeless. The female is crumpled against the passenger door. The hypodermic needle stuck in her arm wobbles as she shakes in spasm. Her eyes and mouth open in horror. I am the last thing she sees as life leaves her eyes.

See Sasquatch and die.

I am not the keeper of these people. No one could ever be.

I am the shadow stalker. A monster.

A myth.

I disappear into the smoke and mist as though I never was.

Chapter Ten

"FRANKLY, YOU'RE annoying us," says Skeknal, one of my older women who is standing at the mouth of a dark cave.

I rub my chest sincerely. "I want to be here when a little one comes into the world."

She shakes her head. "She will show you the child. You know that. We will all rejoice in the presence of new life."

But I feel that I should be at the birth." She isn't buying it. "I should express my feelings for the new child the same way a mother does."

"I've never heard of males asking for this," she says firmly. "What makes you feel this way?"

"A wise one told me this."

"Who? Certainly not Shattuck the Gray. He has been messaging concern about you to all of us."

"What is that old coot concerned about?"

"You and the humans. You know that."

"He need not worry about me. I am the dominant one here. These are my lands. Let me see the child being born."

"Our ways are ancient." She bows respectfully. "Indeed, you are dominant and you have our affection. However, we know our roles as well as you do. The circle of birth is not your place but you may stay at the entrance to the cave. We will bring your child to you soon."

I wait outside the cave, pacing. Once she cited tradition, I had to comply. But I still feel driven by those words, "Love as your mother loved you." Who is sending me these messages?

My mother died years ago after stepping into a metal trap. Her wound became infected and she was gone in a few days. My father took her to the Lake of Souls and mourning howls filled the sky, all the way to the sea.

My father died from injuries he suffered after he defeated another male who tried to claim our domain. So dominant was he that Shattuck himself took him to the Lake. And then Shattuck named me Protector of the Lake and the dominant one here even though many said I was too young.

Many can often be wrong.

Like that man, Vincent Zambelli. I saw him and his fellow protestors screaming at the group home earlier in the day. A large van that has *State of Washington Office for the Disabled* printed on the side delivered some people. Two of the people could hardly walk and needed attendants to guide them into their new home. One was in a wheel chair, flapping his hands the way Christopher does, not comprehending that he is unwanted.

Zambelli shouted at them with his voice machine and his people followed his lead.

Is there no bottom to the human soul? I return my thoughts to the new life that will be brought to me from inside the cave.

Just after dark, the women emerge. A tiny female child is already nursing at her mother's breast.

"She already has your appetite," her mother says with a serene smile.

I caress her face. "You have done well. You honor me and your parents."

"Let us gather in a circle," the older woman says.

We raise the child to the sky and the other women surround us, arms raised. I feel joy—for the first time in a long time - surge through me. *"YAPAAAAH!"*

"YAPAAAAH!" the women shout together.

The forest explodes with howls. Males pound trees with oak all the way to the sea.

This is our way. For thousands of years, we have lived in the shadows of your world. Though we are few, we have survived. We are all connected through time and blood.

But as I reflect on this new life, I realize that some humans have also had to fight for their existence, for their right to live in peace, their right to justice. And as the celebration winds down, I am worried about Christopher. Will he end up like the people in the group home? Will people like Zambelli shout ugly words of hatred at him? Why are others treating him and his mother so ruthlessly?

Despite our moment of joy, my people, like Christopher and his mother, are just hanging on.

Why is it that others don't see the joy that this child brings his mother? I get that he's different, but I haven't met a human yet that wasn't odd. All humans are odd.

But what can I do for him? What can I do for any human other than the Shaman? At least I could replace his rocking chair after I broke it. I think of the couple dying in that car. Why were they there with needles in their arms?

Why was I the last thing the young girl saw before dying? Again, *see me and die.*

How can I do anything for Christopher and his mother when I believe that I can only bring them death?

Late the next night, I pay Two-Moons another visit. He is sleeping in his new rocking chair, covered by the blanket that bears the image of a red bird, wings open. He opens his eyes as I enter.

"I hear that you have a new family member, my hairy brother."

"A female."

He smiles. "Girls can be a hard to raise. Take it from me."

"She will be her mother's problem. I have enough problems right now."

He opens the refrigerator. "You like Chinese food? My daughter brought me some take-out."

I shrug my shoulders. "I eat anything."

He nods as he dumps the food into a pan and lights the flame. "What's troubling you?"

"I fear that I'm cursed. Humans keep dying around me."

The Shaman smiles gently as he stirs the food in the pan. "Well then, I guess I don't have to worry about breakfast tomorrow."

"It doesn't apply to you."

"You really think you're cursed?"

"I fear that I am doomed to wander endlessly upon the earth."

"You've been listening to the white man's ancient stories."

"Their blood cries to the creator."

"So does the blood of my people. So does the blood of yours. The earth is bathed in blood."

"I'm worried about the wandering child. I fear that there will come a day when others treat him the way Zambelli treats the people from the state office for the disabled."

I saw that man on the television. Not from around here. Has no connection to our lands. No respect."

"He hates people who aren't even a threat to him."

"He's using this as a way to get attention. People have always used fear of others to do this." He sprinkles some salt on the food. "You say the child in the cabin wanders?"

"Yes. Even though the town residents don't accept him, they have to go looking for him and it causes them problems."

"He is searching for a greater awareness. There's some heavy magic around him. I can't believe that he's a white child."

"Why do you feel that I should I watch over this child and his mother if I can only bring them death?"

He smiled and nodded. "Because a miracle is going to happen."

"How? What can I do for them? How can I be their keeper?"

He pours the food onto a plate. "I don't know. I am old and maybe I'm crazy."

The Chinese food tastes slimy and odd. "You're not crazy. You need another vision to help me."

"I'm eighty-four years old. I can't do this too much longer, brother. I worry that no one will keep our traditions. Hardly anyone speaks our language any more. Just me and a few others. Someday you'll come here and I'll be gone."

"I don't know where this is all going. I heard the bearded Rabbi in the town speak of the two brothers. But I don't know how their story ends."

"It ends with blood sacrifice. Their traditions have powerful meaning, just as ours do. People don't transform without the shedding of blood."

"Why? I don't understand."

"People forget the old stories but I remember them. Our ancestors came to our lands from far away. To get here we had to walk the mountain trails. We had to make sacrifices. Finally, we saw the land of the Red Cedar and the Thunderbird, a land that provides everything anyone could ever need." Two-Moons shook his head. "Before it was taken away."

"But you have some of your lands again."

"Just some. And elders like Billy Frank had to make great sacrifices to get back what we could."

"Is another great sacrifice coming?"

"Lately I feel the Thunderbird stirring. People keep desecrating the earth. Keep desecrating each other. The tribal council says we have to move our village to higher ground. They say it's flooding due to climate change, but I know what it really is. We've stirred the wrath of the Thunderbird. People will not listen. And so, the waters rise."

"I need to know why I am *this* boy's keeper."

"What does he speak of? What does he say?"

"He doesn't. He can't talk."

He stood up from his chair. "What?"

"The child can't speak. He has no words. His mother says that he has never spoken a single word."

Two-Moon's eyes opened wide in astonishment. "He's been talking to *you* my brother. I saw that in the vision." He touched my hand, suddenly possessed with enormous strength and starred out the window of the cabin. "And I'm seeing that now!"

"But that would mean..."

"Go!"

I bolted from the cabin and tore through the woods. The sky was filled with a looming heaviness. Thunder shook the forest. Lightning streaked across the sky.

Dawn was breaking and was I risking being seen. But I had to find the boy. Visions of him wandering through the woods filled my mind.

I saw a hawk circling above the trees. Hawks never fly in a thunderstorm. All nature felt disturbed.

I leaped over a road and ran up an embankment, barely avoiding a car that screeched to a halt and slammed into the guard rail.

I could hear Sheriff LaHood's voice blasting through the woods from a voice machine like the one Zambelli used.

"Christopher! Just stand still so we can find you. Your mother wants you home."

The forest was filled with humans. They were shouting and calling for the boy. The rain was pouring down and thunder rattled the valleys.

In my mind, I could hear Marianna crying as she did that night in Christopher's bedroom.

In my mind I saw Christopher wandering toward the edge of a valley, the hawk looming in the sky above him. There was a steep cliff ahead. If he kept going, he would fall hundreds of feet to his death.

And yet his eyes, his peaceful, blue eyes, looked right through me.

The vision of him falling filled me with dread.

It had become day light. The woods were full of humans with guns, desperately trying to find the wandering boy in the heavy rain.

I was risking my life. I was risking the discovery of my people. I am not this child's keeper. I am not this child's parent. I am not even of this child's race. Why was I running toward this child? I could only bring him death. I am risking my own children.

All those who see me die.

LaHood's voice was getting closer. I could see the lights from the police cars. I heard the wailing sound. More policemen were pouring into the woods as I swung from tree to tree. Even these idiots would see me. I am nine feet tall and I can be seen. They have guns and will shoot me and then the child will die anyway.

I am not this child's keeper. I am not my brother's keeper.

The Thunderbird's scream pierces the clouds as lightning streaks across the sky.

I grab Christopher by his shirt collar just before he plunges off the cliff.

Chapter Eleven

"SHERIFF. WE FOUND the boy!" shouts a voice over one of the radios.

LaHood stops in his tracks a hundred feet from the cliff and pulls his radio out of his rain coat. "Status?"

"He's fine sir—thank God."

"Location?"

"The back seat of your car, sir. Asleep."

The storm had ended. Within a few minutes, all the law enforcement officers are surrounding Christopher and Marianna. I can see all of this happening from high above them, hidden in the thick branches of an ancient pine. The men and women from the search team are rejoicing as Marianna cries and hugs her bewildered son.

LaHood scans the area, perplexed. "Raymond," he says to his deputy, "what do ya' make of this?"

"We got the kid. Thank God."

"You're not gettin' my meanin'. How did the kid end up in my car?"

"I guess you left it open."

"No shit. But nobody noticed him walking by? We had thirty sworn officers runnin' around this place—trained investigators. They all missed this kid wandering past them?" He glared into the deputy's eyes. "There's some bullshit goin' on round here."

"Maybe they couldn't see because of the all the rain." LaHood shook his head at him. "I guess it is odd."

"Yeah, you could say that." He lowered his voice. "After everybody's done celebrating, we're bringin' this pretty blue-eyed park ranger and her feral, maniac kid down to headquarters. I want some answers."

"The kid can't talk."

"I know that, Raymond. But something else is going on here. Somethin' weird."

"There's been a lot whacky stuff lately, sir."

"Now you're hearin' me. I've heard stuff around town about lady blue eyes here havin' a hot and heavy romance. I'm bettin' the guy she's rockin' the mattress with has a history. Let's start there."

"Yes sir."

Another officer was chirping on LaHood's radio. "Sheriff, Winslow here."

LaHood lifted the radio to his mouth. "What d' ya got?"

"Car went off the road on Highway Seventeen."

"Injuries?"

"Bumps and bruises. Nothing major. Nice couple from Renault. They said that they crashed while trying to avoid a Big Foot running across the road."

LaHood rolled his eyes. "I'm sure it was just a bear. Ambulance?"

"They're okay. They just need a tow truck."

"Hey, you know what? Connect them to those morons doing Big Foot research. The TV crew's renting out Wally's old place over on Black Fish Road. Maybe they'll end up on television or something."

"K that, sir."

LaHood walked over to Marianna. "Ranger Carino, we

need you to come to headquarters and help us with some paper work."

"Sure," Marianna replied. "I'm sorry for the trouble we're causing you."

"Trouble's my business. But we need to talk a while."

"Sure. Anything wrong?"

LaHood leaned against his car and folded his arms. "I don't know. You tell me."

"I work in law enforcement, too, Sherriff. If there was nothing to talk about, you wouldn't waste your time."

"Policing a town is a hell of a lot different from checkin' people's fishin' licenses."

"No disrespect, sir, but I've worked my ass off to get this job. I've seen a lot in this wilderness. Found that hunter who fell down a ravine a few months ago. Remember? The one whose head exploded."

"Maxine the M. E. showed me photos. Yeah, that was a bad one. But I got one worse. Some son-of-a-bitch dumped a dead biker with a hole in his forehead on the roof of my cruiser. The man was dead for a week and stunk to hell. That was as revoltin' as it gets."

"I heard. It wasn't me, Sheriff."

LaHood laughed. "Don't worry, I didn't have you in mind as a suspect. Look, I know you're new to the area and that you're tryin' to do the best you can for your son."

"I owe you a debt for searching for him." Marianna looked at him directly. "I'll tell you whatever you need to know, but you already know the time-line on everything that happened here."

"I do hear you got a boy-friend."

Marianna nodded. "I hear you got a wife."

He chuckled then opened the car door. "No doubt about that. Hop in. I'll get you and your son somethin' to eat. Then we'll talk awhile."

I climbed down from the tree after everyone left,

found a secluded spot between some rocks. No one knew of these rocks. They had ancient drawings of the Thunderbird and other symbols on them. I was exhausted and confused from the day's events. My mind was spinning.

Why was I doing the things I was doing?

I dreamed that I was sleeping in a field full of flowers and that my children were playing around me. The sky was deep blue and the sun was bright and warm.

We were all free. Not hunted. Not hiding in the shadows.

Christopher was sniffing the flowers and smiling. He wasn't humming or moaning or flapping his hands the way he usually does. It was as though all of the tension and all the fear had left his soul. His eyes were full of peace. He pointed to the heavens. "The sky shelters us all. We share the sky."

"Are you a Shaman?" I asked him.

"I am who I am. Who are you?"

"I am the protector of my ancestor's spirits in the Lake of Souls."

"The Creator protects all spirits. It is the living who need you."

"Why have you come here?"

Christopher smiled. "To raise you to the sky. Blessed are those who protect the weak, they shall be given the sky."

And I dreamed of the flowers and the blue, blue sky.

Chapter Twelve

HASSELBECK SPOKE INTO the camera that was set up in front of the Town Hall. "We've decided to call a town meeting to see how many of the residents have had Big Foot encounters. Our conversation with the Winkler family, who almost hit a Squatch on Highway 17, convinced us that we are indeed looking at a hot spot here in Deception Falls."

This was going to be a real freak show. I can't wait until Hasselbeck and his fellow researchers see what the town's wackos are really about. I can see through one of the windows that all the seats are filled; camera lights give the old hall an odd glow. LaHood looms in the back with his arms folded watching the proceedings, shaking his head. Mayor Wallace entered and stood next to LaHood. "This will be great for eco-tourism, Jack."

"It's bullshit." LaHood says under his breath.

"People spend good money for bullshit all the time. Why not spend some of it here?"

Hasselbeck sits up front with Rachel, the skeptic, and Mongo, the true believer. He starts the meeting at the podium. "Good evening everybody. I'm Dr. Joseph

Hasselbeck. My team and I are from the North American Primate Research Organization." The crowd applauds.

I'm already pissed off.

"We're looking for information about your experiences with the local Big Foot population. If you have seen a Big Foot yourself, or heard about an encounter, please raise your hand."

Just about everybody raises their hands as the TV camera pans the crowd. LaHood rolls his eyes. He looks over to see Two-Moons entering, his oak cane helping him walk and navigate his way in. His nephew, the one he called Whale-Shit, guides him to a chair in the back.

The first one to get up and speak is Frank. People in town call him "Mad Dog" because he's got the wild-eyed look of a mangy dog and because he tends to be loud and excitable.

"I'm Frank McDougal. I saw a Squatch takin' a leak behind my wood shed 'bout a year ago. Son-of-a-bitch had to be twelve feet tall!" McDougal waves his arms over his head, indicating the enormous size of the beast. "This squatch stunk like hell."

You don't smell too good yourself, you flatulent blowhard.

"He had freaky red, angry eyes. He threw a log at me."

This is a bold-faced lie. If one of us had thrown a log at this psycho, he'd be sleeping with worms. We don't miss.

Rachel looked at Mad Dog with suspicion. "Twelve feet? That's twice as tall as Mongo here."

"Dude, that would be a Squatch world record," Mongo added.

"Okay," Hasselbeck said. "What happened next?"

"He ran into the woods and I chased him for a while."

Rachel nodded then asked, "So, you chased a twelve-foot tall Big Foot after he threw a log at you?" Mad Dog sat down.

This is nonsense. Nobody chases one of us and lives to talk about it at a town meeting.

Hasselbeck shook his head and pointed at a boy. "Okay. How about you? What's your name, son?"

"My name is Shaun McGaffey. I'm twelve. I saw one running across a field toward some woods behind my grand-dad's barn. It was a-ways from me but it seemed to have a smaller one on its back. I think it was a mom one."

"When was this?" Rachel asked.

"About a month ago."

"It ran really fast. I think she was eating some apples off a tree we've got back there."

"Really?" Hasselbeck made a note on a pad. "Would your grandfather allow us on his property?"

"If I ask him. Otherwise he'd shoot you."

Everyone laughed. Then a scary, burly man with crooked eyes stood up. "Speaking of gun fire, I took a shot at one ten years ago out by the Skokum River Gorge. I think I got 'em, too. But I never found the body."

"Why'd you shoot at him?" Rachel asked.

"Been hunting my whole life. Killed every kind of thing you can find in these woods."

"What's your name?" Mongo asked.

"Offit. Ralph Offit."

Another local hunter stood up. "My name is Mike Conroy. I was hunting Elk in 1998 from a small rise next to a game trail when I heard something behind me. Something was moving through the brush. I turned to look at what was there and that's when I saw it. It was huge. It looked at me and stopped. I felt the hair on my neck stand up."

What did you do next?" Hasselbeck asked.

"I turned with the rifle. I was afraid it might charge me."

"Did it charge you?" Mongo asked.

"No. It just slipped back into the brush—glided really.

Never seen nothin' move like that. It was so silent, so powerful. I felt, well, awe. In a second or two, it just vanished into the woods."

"Why didn't you shoot it?" Offit asked.

Tears filled his eyes. "I've been huntin' my whole life. This'll sound strange, but, it was too human, too magnificent. I had no right to shoot it."

Well that was different.

Whap! Whap!

The old Shaman hit one of the beams holding up the balcony with his oak cane. The noise startled everyone in the room and they all turned to see Two-Moons standing, eyes glaring. "Conroy. You Thomas Conroy's son?" Two Moons asked the man who had just spoken.

"Yes sir, I am."

"I knew him. Good person. Your father raised you right. Maybe there is some good left in this world." Two-Moons raised his hand in the air. "This man has seen the spirit of the dark woods and he felt what you should all feel—reverence."

"I'm sorry sir," Hasselbeck said nervously. "What is your name?"

"I am Salli Tani'm—*Two-Moons* in your tongue. I've lived here for eighty-four years in the shadow of Sunh-a-do, the mountain you call *Olympus*. You should stop interfering with the world of C'iatqo."

Hasselbeck stood up. "Sir, we intend to never harm..."

"Your people promised us that before, and still, harm was done. You cannot see a spirit-being with machines."

"Sir, I give you my word, we are scientists."

"Is it not scientists who say that 'there will be no harm from the pipeline'? Is it not scientists who say 'there will be no environmental impact'?"

Hasselbeck sat down.

The Shaman took a few steps down the center aisle and spoke to the audience. "What of respect for the land, the water, the people, our ancestors? Look at what is really going on around you. We are risking the wrath of the Thunderbird. We are desecrating the earth. We are not living as we should and the waters are rising." He tapped his oak walking stick in the floor. "My friend," he said to Hasselbeck, "what you say you are, isn't important. Your actions are. You say that you seek him with peace in your heart?"

Hasselbeck nodded. "I swear it," he said quietly.

"Then come back after you've made sacrifices. Come back, when your heart is pure. Then you may see him." Two-Moons raised his hands. "The Great Spirit reveals only when we have proven we are ready. Until we are, let the spirit of the dark woods live in peace." The Shaman turned and left the room, Whale-Shit following him.

Everyone sat stunned.

The meeting wound down, so I moved onto Christopher's house. The boyfriend was back and he'd brought flowers. Marianna stood on the porch, glaring at the red-bearded muscular man. "You think some roses will make up for not telling me the truth?"

"I'm hoping that they'll at least give me a chance to explain," he said. "It's not like I wasn't gonna tell you."

"Clint, I have a job in law enforcement and I really need it. I have a son with special needs. You know that I need the state benefits."

"Darlin', I was gonna tell you."

"But you didn't. I had to hear it from LaHood. You should've told me that you'd done time."

"I was younger and way more stupid than I am now."

"You're still not that smart."

"Maybe I ain't." Clint looked down at his feet. "But I fell hard for you. It isn't easy to live with a record in a small town, people lookin' at you all the time. It ain't easy bein' half-free."

Marianna took the flowers and looked Clint in the eyes. "LaHood says I need to be careful around you."

"I hate him, but he's right."

Marianna step back.

"LaHood didn't lie to you. I made mistakes and I paid for them. I just want to think right and live right. I've fallen head over heels for you and I can't think right if I think 'bout losing you. Please don't turn away from me."

The couple embraced.

I went to check on Christopher and found him already asleep. I went back to my sleeping hole between the rocks with the bird paintings on them.

I woke at dawn to hear the sounds of humming and feet rustling the leaves on the forest floor. It was Christopher. Once again, he had wandered out of his house. He was carrying a flower for some reason.

Here we go again.

I rose quietly, staying hidden from him. Once he walked past me, I knew that I'd have to stop him again from going over the cliff, so I got up and silently followed.

Christopher meandered onto a game trail then turned to see me looming over him. "Hairy man, I've been looking for you."

I knew it.

Christopher could mind speak.

Chapter Thirteen

CHRISTOPHER SMILED and flapped his hands. The nine-year-old was smiling from ear to ear. "You can mind speak," I messaged back.

"And you can hear me. You're the only one who can."

"How did you learn to do this? I've never heard the minds of other humans."

"Neither have I, but I've always felt them."

"I suppose I have, too. I have to consider that."

Christopher handed me the rose. He must have taken it from the flowers that his mother received from her boyfriend. "I am so happy not to be alone anymore. You're the first person I've ever spoken too."

I studied the flower. It glowed deep red. The smell was intoxicating. "I'm hardly a person to your kind. They call me things like *primate* or *wild man*. And then they hunt me for personal glory. Only you have called me a person."

"They give me labels, too. Many believe I am too different to be a real person. I guess that is why the creator wanted us to meet. This is what we share, along with the sky."

"I'm not sure that it was the Creator. I'm not sure he listens to us."

"It is we who aren't listening for him. The Creator is all around us, but people do not see this."

"You are a Shaman."

"I am who I am."

"You shouldn't come out here alone. It is dangerous in the woods."

"I am never alone. I have you and I have the Creator. I have all that I need."

"But you need to be careful. You almost fell off that cliff yesterday."

"I knew you would save me. Why did you make me fall asleep after you caught me?"

"It is something my kind learned to do thousands of years ago to keep people from remembering that they'd seen us. We have to make people forget or they will come back with others to hunt us. We are few. We must live in the shadows."

"I have also lived in the shadow cast by the fears of others." He put his hand on my hand. His touch vibrated energy. "Blessed are those who overcome the shadows, they shall be filled with light."

"Let's get you home. I don't want your mother to wake up and panic." I picked him up and carried him on my back. He held on tightly. I got him through his bedroom window a few minutes later.

"That was a fun ride," he said. "I have to go see my teachers soon."

I nodded. "It is you who is a teacher. It was good to talk."

I stayed in the woods for a while and watched the cabin. A short time later, Christopher walked out to his bus with his mother and got in. I saw him looking for me.

"I am here," I messaged him.

Marianna received a phone call when she got back inside. Her boss needed her to work a second shift and keep a closer eye on the parking area where the two young people had died in their cars. Marianna hung up the phone and turned to her boyfriend.

Hidden by some bushes outside the cabin, I peered into the room and listened to the couple.

"Clint, I need a favor."

"Whatever you need," he said as he got dressed.

She poured a cup of coffee. "Can you watch Christopher tonight? I have to work a double."

"I will, but I don't know if he'll like that."

"He'll be okay. I'll have dinner ready because he's on a special diet. He's got a new favorite video and that should help for one night."

Clint took the coffee. "I'll do my best."

"Just make sure that he doesn't walk out the front door. I can swing by and check in on him a couple of times during my shifts. I have to keep an eye on the folks parking at the Saddle Brook Lot."

"Hickey Point."

"Why do the locals call it that?"

"Because that's where the old mayor's daughter got a hickey on her neck a while back."

"Who gave her the hickey?"

"Now what kinda' man talks about past relationships?"

She sat on his lap. "A scoundrel like you does."

They kissed. "I'll take care of him, darlin'. Then I'll be waiting for you here."

I needed to know if others could mind speak with humans. The only non-human who was around humans all day was that idiot, Tang, at the county zoo. I went there to see what he was up to.

As usual, Tang was sitting on the branch of his artificial tree. He was eating some kind of fruit watching Orenstein mix something into his food dish. Humans walked around the park but they couldn't see me from my perch in the woods.

"Tang."

Nothing.

"Tang!"

More nothing.

"Tang, I'm going to break in and steal your fruit!"

"Why would you do such a thing?"

"I see I have your attention, finally."

"There's no need to pay attention, unless someone threatens your food supply."

"You've been getting more shots from that grey-haired, white-coated human, haven't you? You seem even stupider than the last time I saw you."

He yawned and stretched out on the branch. "I'm not stupid. I'm content. Why do you hate this place?"

"Because it's a prison."

"It's a zoo. They take care of me here."

I wanted to bash his skull in. "It's got bars. You're not free to go. You don't see the humans simply accept being jailed. I've seen them fight and protest when LaHood and his deputies take them into police headquarters."

"Does LaHood feed them?"

"I don't know. I guess so. They're given lawyers and are brought before Judge Holland. I've listened to their proceedings."

"What's the point of this questioning? I need to pee."

"The point is that even stupid humans fight for their freedom." Tang turned and urinated. "Whatever. I have a question."

"You always seem to have another one."

"Can you mind speak with the humans who visit you?"

"No. Should I?"

"Have you ever heard their thoughts?"

"No. I've always been happy to let them look and point at me. I don't think anyone's ever cared to communicate with me."

"So, you've never had this experience."

"No. We have routines and procedures around here and we follow them. That's all that ever matters. I do know that they are bringing me a female next week, though. I heard the white coat talking about it. The good times roll next week!"

"I can break you and your woman free if you want. We'll find a place for both of you somewhere out here. You don't have to stay in this hell hole."

"We'll be fine here. No thanks."

Well, Tang hadn't changed. I would have to tell Shattuck the Gray what was happening. Maybe he would have an answer.

I went to the top of a tree deep in the forest and messaged Shattuck.

But he wouldn't answer me.

Chapter Fourteen

SHATTUCK THE GRAY was pissing me off and I was getting frustrated. No matter how many times I messaged him, he wouldn't reply. Why?

It was time to put a little more energy into my surveillance of the town's despicable residents. I went to see the home for the disabled and once again there were people protesting around it. But I was surprised to see that the priest was there talking to some of the protesters about caring for those in the home. Zambelli and his people stood silently. "I am asking all of you to remember that Jesus told us to love each other."

Zambelli continued to shake his head.

Then I went to the temple of the Jews. The rabbi began his sermon by saying that he agreed with the priest and that people should accept the group home.

"We must remember that our people have been persecuted wherever we have lived. We have a moral obligation to be accepting of others."

I really liked the rabbi and the way he told stories from their past. I gather that the Jewish tribe has been around for a long time.

This evening's story was about a man named Abraham who was told by God to take his son to the top of a mountain, bind him, kill him, and burn his body as a sacrificial offering—heavy stuff. I nearly fell through a stained-glass window in as I leaned against the building. Where was the rabbi going with this?

Right as Abraham was about to plunge the dagger into his son, God sends an angel to stop him. I didn't see that one coming. It seems that their God didn't require Abraham to slay his children to satisfy him.

Once again, the rabbi had me wondering. What was the point of this story? What kind of God sets you up for an ordeal like this, then stops you at the last minute? Why would anyone sacrifice children for a religion?

At least their God stopped the insanity. But humans never stop their insanity. As I move through the autumn darkness on the edge of the town I see that the man who sells the products that humans inject into themselves is back at work. He must not have heard the story of Abraham. He lets people sacrifice themselves.

The man from the alley walks out under the street light. Right on cue, a car rolls up. Money and a package were exchanged. I see a couple in the car. The car drove away into the hills, just as the dead couple had done.

This man from the alley is peddling death from a syringe—for money. If the God of the Jews won't send an angel, whatever that is, to stop this monster, then maybe I have to do it. I don't really need all these human entanglements in my life, but maybe this is what the rabbi was getting to.

I moved down the hill, seething. I gathered some rocks into a pile behind a line of young pine trees and waited.

I didn't have to wait long.

A pick-up truck flashed its headlights and began slowing down. The white man from the alley emerged again with a big, greedy smile on his face.

The man in the car spoke. "Got some?"

"Always," said the man from the alley. "Best shit in town."

I decided to send a warning. *"Whoooup. Whoooup."*

The white man peered over the roof of the car. "What the hell was that?"

The man in the car looked around nervously. "You heard cops?"

"No, it was like an animal or somethin'."

"Give me the stuff. Here's the money."

"Whoooup! Whoooup!"

I fired a rock that slammed into the rear of the truck.

The man in the truck was livid. "Who the ..."

"Who's screwing with my corner?" The white man yelled.

"WHAAAAHOOOO!"

The man in the car peered out through his window. "What the hell is that?"

"Come out of the bushes, you punk!" The white man screamed.

I aimed for the driver's side window and fired a bigger rock. *Blam!* The glass shattered into hundreds of tiny splinters.

The man from the alley was now wide-eyed. "What the..."

"Ahhh! Ahhh!" The man in the car screamed. "Shards! My eyes! Ahhh!" He accelerated into a turn but couldn't see what he was doing. He slammed into a parked car on my side of the street. A giant bag exploded into his face, knocking him unconscious.

"Who threw the rock?" The man from the alley took out a gun and began firing into the woods. "Who's screwing with my corner?" he shouted, firing more rounds as he crossed into the middle of the street. A round burned through a branch near my head.

This was now a matter of self-defense. *"AHHWHOOO!"*

I fired a jagged rock with vicious intent. It plowed into his groin and he fell to floor, writhing in agony.

"Oh God!" he moaned, rolling around in the broken glass in the middle of the street. His gun tumbled onto the road next to him.

I could hear the police cars coming, with lights shining and sirens wailing away. Within a few moments, one of LaHood's deputies screeched to a stop, thirty feet from the man in the street. The deputy got out of his car, gun drawn.

"Who did this to me?" the man yelled, holding onto his guts. He was enraged and didn't notice the deputy as he picked up his gun, pointing it my direction to fire again.

"Police! Drop the gun!"

The man turned toward the officer. It was the last thing that he would ever do. The officer opened fire.

He collapsed, dead in the road. Rolls of money and the packages he sold mixed with his blood on the damp pavement.

More deputies poured onto the scene as I worked my way up the embankment, deeper into the woods.

The deputy who shot the man was distraught. He crumpled in shock behind his car. "It happened so fast," he told the other deputies.

"You done good, Winslow," another deputy said. We got your back. He was a drug dealer and the guy's gun is right there, next to him on the street."

"He gave me no choice. I had to shoot."

Some deputies attempted to help the dead man but it was too late. Others helped the man in the car wreck. Within a few minutes, LaHood arrived, seething. "What the hell happened?!"

The deputies reported what they knew to LaHood. The man who was in the truck regained consciousness as the medical workers moved him onto the stretcher toward the ambulance.

"Hold him a minute," LaHood barked.

"Sheriff, we gotta get this man to the ER or he's gonna lose his eyes."

"I said hold him til I ask a question."

"Sheriff, we got to move him now."

LaHood glared at the medical man. "This is my town. I got an officer in shock who had to kill a man. I'm asking this puke-ball a question."

"All right. Make it quick."

"Who was that bastard shooting at before my deputy got here?"

"I don't know."

"Don't give me that, punk, or I'll rub the glass deeper into your eye balls!"

"Sheriff!" the medical man shouted.

"It was an animal!"

"What?"

"It was a freakin' animal!"

"Don't bullshit me!"

"I swear to God! It made some sort of whooping sound. It was throwing rocks at us. Then my window exploded. I freaked out and crashed my car."

The man was taken away. The scene was cordoned off with yellow tape and LaHood directed his men to ask the people in the two apartments overlooking the scene to give reports.

A while later, Deputy Raymond approached LaHood after receiving a phone call. "Sheriff, I got somethin' odd here."

"Raymond, this whole damn town's getting' odd."

"McKenzie, the drug dealer, had a large jagged rock embedded in his guts. The E.R surgeon says that he was gonna die from that wound anyway. His innards were ripped beyond repair. Winslow just put 'em out of his misery."

"So, this wasn't a gun fight?"

"No. We don't know what it was."

LaHood walked out to the middle of the street and looked up into the woods.

Chapter Fifteen

MOVING ALONG TO other parts of the realm, the couple who bought drugs had indeed parked in the Saddle Brook lot. But they weren't dead like the last couple I saw there. The man, who had crazed eyes, was trying to force himself on the woman and she wasn't willing. He was victimizing her in the car. I'd heard this happen in the town between other couples and it made my guts twist.

No male should ever do this to a female. This kind of behavior is inconceivable to my people. We don't even have a word for it.

This was turning out to be a bad night. It was as if the biker gangs had returned.

The young woman was crying in agony and terror. It was time to act. I broke a thick tree branch and fashioned it quickly into a club. My plan was simple: bash the man's skull in with one swing and then erase the woman's memory.

I was about to leave the woods and move toward the car when I saw headlights stream into the parking lot. It was Marianna in her Ranger vehicle.

I moved back into the woods.

Marianna quickly pulled to a stop and got out of her car. She activated a device that worked like LaHood's voice amplifier. "People, step out of the car."

I could see the man holding his hand over the woman's mouth as she tried to scream. He was preventing her from leaving the vehicle. Marianna couldn't see what I was seeing due to the glare from her headlights.

"Exit the vehicle—now!"

The woman broke away from the man and bolted from the car. "He raped me!" she screamed. She turned to run for Marianna's vehicle but tripped. The man fell on top of her and dragged her back to his car in a head lock. He had a gun.

Another man with a gun.

"Screw with me and I'll blow her brains out!" He smacked her in the head with the weapon, leaving her moaning and semi-conscious. Blood oozed down the woman's forehead.

Marianna drew her gun. She was shaking, but she spoke clearly into her radio. "Ranger Carino requires Deception Falls Sheriff's assistance. Saddle Brook Lot, Cascadia Park, West Entrance. Young female claims that a tall, white male has raped her. The male has a gun and has pistol whipped the woman. He is refusing to release her from a white Ford Taurus in the south end of the lot. Washington license, TGQ-599." Marianna kept her revolver aimed as she spoke through the loud speaker. "Let the woman go, throw the gun out the window and step clear of the vehicle." She directed a floodlight onto the vehicle.

The man stepped out of the driver's side door and shouted over the roof of the car. "Screw you! Get the hell out of here or I'll kill her then come for you."

"Mister, I'm not going anywhere," Marianna responded. "You're leaving this parking lot in hand cuffs. You hurt this woman anymore and you'll leave in a box."

Boy, Christopher's mother was one courageous lady. This thug was ten inches taller than she was, nasty and violent. And Marianna wasn't backing down.

He pointed his gun toward Marianna. "I'll do you, too, lady. You sure look pretty."

Marianna kept her door open to provide some cover. "I'm not having it that way, mister."

Shoot this criminal! Blow his brains out! I wanted to scream. I realized, though, that Marianna was concerned that an exchange of gun fire might wound the woman, too. She was really in a tough spot. I searched for another sharp, jagged rock.

Marianna's steely voice boomed over the loud speaker. "I'm going to say this again, throw the gun toward me and let the girl go. Then step clear of the vehicle."

"You aint got what it takes to shoot me. I'm gonna come for you."

"No, you're not," she responded.

"Yeah? Who's gonna stop me, bitch?"

He really shouldn't have said that.

The man's head lurched forward as a chunk of his brains splattered onto the roof of the car. He slumped against the car door, blood spewing from his open skull, and slid to the cold gravel floor of the parking lot. His legs shook in a death spasm. The woman in the car screamed in horror and shock.

"What the hell?" Marianna's eyes darted around the parking lot.

A voice came over the radio. "Ranger Carino, this is dispatch. Status?"

"Man down. Need medical assistance."

She moved toward the vehicle, shaking, gun focused on the spot where the man lay dead. I could see the steam from Marianna's breath hang in the air. The woman in the car was screaming uncontrollably. Marianna stood over the dead man. She gasped and looked as though she might vomit, but steadied herself. "Come out of the car, honey. He's dead."

"Oh my God!"

Marianna held out her hand. "It's over. You're safe now."

"You saved my life. I didn't even hear you shoot him."

"I didn't shoot him. His head just... exploded."

The woman clung to Marianna as they walked back to Marianna's vehicle. Marianna held the woman and steered her from looking at the carnage. "Don't look."

"How'd you do that to him?"

Marianna continued to scan the parking lot. "I didn't. Sit in my car. I can hear the Sheriff's people coming. It's over and you're going to be okay." She used the floodlight to scan the lot and the woods that enclosed them. I moved deeper into the brush so she couldn't see me.

"My stuff is in the car."

"Leave it there. This is a crime scene now."

"We were doing heroin. He went crazy and raped me. I couldn't push him off. I thought that he was a cool guy."

"It's okay." Marianna cleared hair from the woman's blood streaked face. "You're young and people make mistakes. And doing heroin is one hell of a mistake."

The girl sobbed. "I'm so ashamed."

"I know. But you didn't deserve what he did to you. No one does. Let me get some bandages for you."

The deputies poured into the lot. Deputy Raymond approached Marianna first. "This has been a bad night already, Carino. What happened here?"

"The couple came up here and did heroin. The dead guy figured he was entitled to sex, I guess, but the girl said no. So, he raped her. I got here and it became a stand-off. We're screaming at each other from our cars." Marianna bent over. Deputy Raymond put his hand on her shoulder to steady her. "I'm thinking that I'm going to have to ventilate this bastard." She looked up at Raymond. "Then his head just blew open."

Deputy Raymond went to look at the dead man. When he saw the man's brains strewn across the roof of the car, he ran to edge of the woods and puked.

LaHood arrived a few minutes later, completely pissed off. "You shot the son-of-a-bitch?"

"No, I didn't," Marianna said.

"So, who did then?"

"I don't know."

LaHood took in the scene. "Been here twenty-five years and never had deadly force events. Now I've had two in one night."

"Sheriff, I never fired a shot."

"We're gonna have to take your gun."

"I'm telling you, I never fired a shot."

"Half his head's missin'. Somebody blew his brains out. You sayin' someone else shot him?"

"I never heard gun fire. All of a sudden his brains erupted all over the roof of the car."

"Sir," Deputy Raymond interrupted.

"Not now, Raymond," LaHood barked.

"Carino couldn't have done this, sir. The wound was in the back of the head and the splatter shows that whatever hit him came from behind him."

LaHood moved around the vehicle and turned back toward Marianna. "Were you by your car?" He pointed at Marianna. "Did you move your car? Is that where your car was?"

"Yeah, I didn't move anything. I know about not altering crime scenes."

LaHood looked at the woman, now shaking under a blanket in the back seat of Marianna's car. She nodded in agreement. He walked around at the scene, looking into both cars with a flashlight. "You're sayin' you didn't shoot him?"

"That's what I'm saying. He was a nasty creep and I was sure ready to."

"He was a creep," the woman shouted from inside Marianna's car.

LaHood nodded. "Well he's a dead creep now. And whoever did this, did it from the woods."

Chapter Sixteen

IT HAD BEEN some night so I wandered back to the Ranger's Cabin and camped out underneath Christopher's window. He was asleep inside. Clint was up, drinking beer and watching TV.

Sheriff LaHood's car rolled up the driveway to the cabin. He was dropping Marianna off at her cabin.

"You gonna be all right?" LaHood asked.

"I'm fine. Wish I understood what happened in that parking lot," Marianna said.

LaHood ran his hand through his hair. "Me, too." He drank some water from a bottle. "What a night. Wish I understood what was happenin' 'round here. I had one of the worst mass homicides in Washington State history at that biker's bar. Half my motor fleet got trashed. Mayor says it's gonna cost the town a fortune. Then tonight's mayhem."

"Well, my situation was outside of the town, so you're not really the responsible agency."

"Yeah, but we got there first so we're gonna get stuck with the investigation. I know how the State Police work. We'll get you your gun and car back at some point tomorrow.

No worries." He drank a little more water. "Job's been a nightmare lately. Getting too old for this shit."

She zipped her jacket up. "I'm sorry. I haven't been much help."

LaHood turned toward Marianna. "You kiddin' me? You're about the toughest lady I ever met. Whatever the hell happened in that parking lot, you saved that girl's life."

"I was doing what I'm supposed to."

"You did more than that."

"I'd ask you in for a drink but my boyfriend's here and it might be awkward.'

"Gave up drinkin' twenty years ago."

"You've seen some dark times, haven't you?"

LaHood drank some more water. "I have. Gives insight into people. You're a good woman. Your boyfriend treatin' you right?"

"So far, so good."

"Tell 'em he'd better, or he'll answer to me. Oh, nearly forgot. Here's my spare duty weapon. This way you'll have something till we get your firearm back to you. Go get some rest, Ranger Carino."

"Thanks, Sheriff. You get some rest, too." Marianna walked up onto the porch and into the cabin. I heard her burst into tears.

"You look like hell," Clint said.

"I saw some creep's brains explode. A seventeen-year-old girl got raped and I have to go through an investigation that's going to have questions I can't begin to answer."

"I'm sorry. I should get going."

"You've been drinking. Stay here. Leave in the morning."

"Why were you talkin' to LaHood?"

"Because he's the Sheriff, because he's going to be handling this investigation and because they had to take my car and gun. That's why."

"I think he's got the hots for you."

"Please don't give me the jealousy stuff right now."

"I'm just sayin'."

"Clint, not now."

It would be dawn soon. Marianna and Clint went to different rooms to sleep. Once all the lights went out, I went to my sleeping hole. I made some improvements to it by putting down some pine branches and leaves. I covered the space between the rocks with more branches and fell asleep.

I woke just before dawn to hear Christopher walking through the leaves. "I never asked your name," he said. "The Creator has a name for all of his children."

"Someday I won't wake up and you'll wander into trouble. That could've been today. I'm exhausted—it was a rough night."

"Mommy's exhausted. She needs her rest."

"Yes, she does. Your mother is like my women. She has great courage."

Christopher started picking up leaves and shredding them. "I'm worried about Clint. He has anger that he can't control."

"I've had that."

"And yet you try to help people."

I looked down. "It occurs to me lately that perhaps I've been overly harsh in my judgments of humans."

Christopher sat down on a rock. "It's important to understand your own faults so that you can understand others."

"How is it that you're so wise?"

"I listen to people. Because they've never heard me speak, they assume that I can never talk about them."

"Same for me."

"Some speak about me as though I'm not even there. But my mommy and my teachers know that I am a person. They talk to me with respect and work hard to be kind."

"These are good people. I wish I saw more like them."

"Blessed are they who are kind, even when no one else sees them being kind."

I handed him some leaves so that he could gently shred them. He seemed to like doing that. "Why is it that you can't speak the same way other humans do?"

"My mother believes I was injured by a drug when I was a baby. But I don't know. It's beyond my memories. I've always been this way."

Drugs again. Humans and their drugs.

I touched his hand and once again felt his incredible energy. "I'm not sure that I really understand myself or that I've overcome my anger."

"To overcome anger, you must help people in need, even when doing so is at great cost."

"What do you do when people look at you and don't seem willing or able to see you as a person?"

"I look to God to stir compassion in my brothers and sisters to see our shared humanity. I ask God for the strength to rise when others would knock me down, to speak when others would impose silence, and love when others would hate. This is what I do."

I nodded. "Those are beautiful words."

"I wish that I could speak them aloud."

"Perhaps someday you will. I will think about them."

"I want you to show me the sky as the sun rises over the mountains."

"This is what we do when our children are born. Climb on my back."

I carried Christopher through the woods, up a ridge. He laughed all the way. When we got to the top, I lifted him over my head.

Christopher's shined with joy as we arrived at the top of the ridge.

The sun rose a moment after I raised him up. *"YAP-AAAAH!"* I shouted loud enough for all to hear.

I carried him home on my back, handing him leaves to shred as we walked through the woods. His face glowed with the red blush of that rose he showed me. "You remind me of that flower you showed me—glowing and peaceful."

"The sunrise was great. The creator lights the world every day."

"Thank you for reminding me how beautiful it is. It is like a dream."

"What do you dream of?"

"Walking without fear under a blue sky."

His eyes focused on mine. "You didn't answer my question."

"What question was that?"

"What is your name?"

"I am Sasquatch." I put him back through his window a few seconds before his mother walked into the room.

"Time to wake up...oh, you're up already. Christopher, do you have gas? The room smells sort of funky. How did those leaves get in here?"

I needed to speak with Shattuck the Gray but his silence continued. "Why won't you answer me, gray one?"

Silence.

"What have I done wrong?"

Chapter Seventeen

RACHEL, THE SKEPTICAL one, is moving quietly through the woods with her backpack on. From time to time, she sets the camera up and says a few words.

"I've been following some animal trails, looking for tracks," she says cheerfully for the camera. "I've seen deer, elk, and bear tracks, but no Big Foot tracks."

That would be because we don't use the pathways that other animals use. When you're nine feet tall, you go wherever you want to.

"The woods can play tricks on you. Joey got spooked a while back on a solo trip out here."

He got more than spooked lady. He needed to change his pants after what I did to him.

"The quiet can trick you into believing that you're being followed."

And sometimes you are.

"I'm looking for a good place to camp where I can have a panoramic view of everything around me. This way I can get a good look at any giant cryptids approaching me—if they really exist."

I guess that I'm a *cryptid*—whatever that is. But guess what, my cute little camper? I'm not going to approach you, even if you tear your clothes off and howl at the moon. I always keep obstructions—trees, bushes full of poison ivy and oak—between me and Big Foot hunters like you. I know my domain and you don't; I can watch you, and you'll never see me.

Rachel sets the camera up by a stream flowing into a large pond. "This place is somewhat open. Best I could find. I'll make camp here because water resources always draw wildlife."

It doesn't take long for her to pitch her tent and start a fire. It's a crisp autumn night and a full moon rises as she cooks some meat on the fire. The smell is intoxicating, but I ate well today so I'm not tempted to play any games. I want my little skeptic to stay my little skeptic. A little while later, she says a few more words into the camera. "I'm going to try what Mongo and Joey call, *girl screams*. They say that the screams of a female sometimes elicit responses from a Big Foot."

Everything that a female does elicits a response from me. Rachel clearly doesn't know my job description. I hunt. I fish. I eat. I protect the domain. Then I make magic with women and produce little hairy breast-sucklers. That's the job of a dominant male. Dealing with humans is not part of the job.

"*Yaaah! Yaaah!*" she screams.

I bury my face in my hands. Now I get why a screaming woman would elicit a response. It was the most annoying noise I've ever heard.

Rachel listens a moment for a response. "Well, no action tonight. I'm going to pack it in and get some sleep. I plan to rise before dawn and make some more noise then. Maybe that's a better time for finding Big Foot."

Okay. I'll hang around these parts for the night. Rest assured Rachel is not finding me tonight.

The moon is full and love magic is in the air. I'm going to visit a lady friend over the rise and then come back to check on Rachel.

Women will be the death of me. Well, something's got to kill you.

Just after sunrise, I hear Rachel screaming. But it's not because she's trying to draw the attention of a Big Foot. Animals are fleeing the area as I tear through the woods to the scene.

A large male brown bear is thrashing the tent to get at Rachel, ripping at the canvass with his claws. My little skeptic will soon be mauled to death. Then the bear will devour her over the course of a few days.

Well that kind of sucks. I liked her.

"Help! Ahhh! Ahhh!"

The bear really has her now. He's got her by the leg and is pulling the torn remains of the tent away from her. Equipment and supplies are flung all over the camp site. Rachel was correct about the water drawing wild life.

It can be bad to be right.

The bear just about has her free of the tent now. The terror in her eyes leaves me feeling queasy. This is hard to watch. Within a few seconds, he will likely chomp down on her throat and rip. Dominant male brown bears know their stuff—you don't get to be dominant without knowing and executing perfect technique.

This is going to be grisly, no pun intended.

To my surprise, Rachel grabs the camera tripod and starts swinging. The big guy didn't see that coming. This lady has character. What a fighter! At least she will die fighting.

I know what you're thinking. I can stop this.

But it's not my place to alter the ways of the woods.

Rachel knew the risks of her research. She understood what she was doing. And I respect her for that. I will announce to all of my kind that Rachel the skeptic, died well.

Her leg is in bad shape but she's still swinging that camera tripod. She smacked the big guy a good one in the chops. He's really pissed now and he's moving in. This is over in a few more seconds.

"Get away from me, you bastard!"

She's still whacking away with the tripod. What courage! What resolve! He has her leg pinned with his claws. It's just about over.

"Blessed are they who are kind, even when no one else sees them being kind."

Oh, damn it to hell.

"WAAAAAH!" I burst from bushes and stand in front of the bear.

Rachel's looks up, amazed. "Oh my God!"

The bear stands his ground. *"EYAAH!"*

I lock eyes on the bear. *"WAAAAAH!"* I rip the tripod out of Rachel's hands and wave it over my head. I tower over the bear as only a giant, hairy, wild man can. *"WOOOOOOO!"*

The bear eases back. I rip open a container of supplies and a package of meat rolls onto the floor. I kick it to the bear. He growls again but takes the meat and runs into the forest.

Now, Rachel is screaming at me, trying to scramble away even though she can't walk. "Oh my God! Help! Help!"

I understand that this may be overwhelming for her. "You should shut up and conserve your strength." She looks at me in astonishment and passes out.

Now what? I've got a wounded female skeptic who will soon bleed to death in the middle of the woods. What the hell am I supposed to do with her? If I leave her here, I am going to worry that the curse has returned: Once again, I will be the last thing that a human sees before leaving this world.

I don't need all this commotion in my life. I have a lot going on. More children on the way. Women summoning me every other night. Shattuck the Gray giving me the silent treatment and investigating me. An angry sheriff who can't keep his town safe. Hasselbeck's people stalking my every move and a kid who can't talk and keeps wandering off his property.

And now this.

I should have let the woods decide this matter. I shouldn't have involved myself.

I fling the skeptic on my back and tear ass to the base camp set up by the North American Primate Research Organization.

The site is deserted. They must be out looking for Rachel—or me.

"Oh God." Rachel moans. "I'm hallucinating from blood loss."

"That's right little one. You're just hallucinating."

"You can talk. Mongo said that he heard Big Foot chatter once. I didn't believe him."

"Why not?"

"I thought he was smoking marijuana. You smell so odd."

"So, do you."

"I'm going to die and I won't be able to tell them about you. Joey was right. The native Americans were right."

"Right about what?"

"You are like a God. But I won't be able to tell them because I'm dying."

"No, you won't be able to tell them because I will erase your memory of me." I held the palm of my hand to her forehead and closed my eyes. My presence left her mind. She passed out again. "You will die someday my little skeptic, but not on this day."

I placed her in the back of one of the pick-up trucks. I needed to summon the others so I ripped a car door off to trigger an alarm. Then I fled to the woods.

Hasselbeck and the others quickly returned. "Oh my God! Get the first aid kit."

Mongo jumped into the rear of the truck. "She's in shock, lost a lot of blood."

A camera man pointed at his damaged car. "What the hell happened to the car door?"

"Never mind that now," Mongo screamed. "Get me some fresh bandages. I'm keeping pressure on her wounds."

"Hold on, Mongo," Hasselbeck shouted. "We're going to drive her to the hospital. She'll die here if we wait here for an ambulance."

Mongo pulled Rachel close to him. "I got her. Burn rubber."

A crew member tossed a blanket into the rear of the truck as they headed out on the dirt road. Mongo lifted Rachel to wrap the blanket around her.

That's when he saw it.

"She's got a giant bloody hand print on her back!"

Oh crap.

Chapter Eighteen

"SHATTUCK, I NEED to talk to you."

Nothing.

"It is critical. Something has happened and I need to advise you. It could change the way we interact with the humans."

Silence.

"If I have to, I will come to you."

"Do not come here. You have exposed all of us to terrible danger. Go deep into the woods. Avoid the humans. You're assigned sacred responsibilities to protect the souls of our ancestors. Remember your place!"

"The child wanders. He will come looking for me and he will get killed if I'm not here."

"What of it? Let him die. You said that we should kill them all."

"But things have changed and I am the only one who can...." I felt the communication terminate.

I had to explain to Shattuck that this child is different. What it all meant, I did not know. But that's why I needed to talk to him.

I went to see the Shaman as a light snow fell quietly

in the forest. He was placing a log in his fire place when I quietly entered his cabin. "I know you are here, my friend. Please make yourself warm by my fire."

"How goes things?"

"They go. My daughter says that I should go to a home. She fears that I will die here."

"This is your home. Why leave?"

He took some food out of the refrigerator and poured it into a pan on the stove. "I'm with you on this. Told her that I will certainly die here. She need not fear that. This is where I want to live and where I want to die."

"We should all be allowed to die on our own terms."

"Few are that lucky. Seek a good death, do you?"

"My father died well. I want the same. I am weary of this world."

"The older we get and lose loved ones, more weary of life, we grow." He held his hands over the fire. "I think we're depressing each other."

"I am not sure what to do about the boy. He can do the mind speak."

Two-Moons stirred the food in the pan. "Got some beef stew for you. The boy is going to be a powerful Shaman. You know, I can only sense you and your kind. I can feel your lives, your heartbreaks and joys. They come to me in visions and dreams. But if you didn't talk as humans do, I would only know you from dreams."

"The boy is different."

"He has entered your life—and our world—for some reason. I'm amazed that he's a white child. Does he have any Chinook in him?"

"I don't know. His mother is white, but could have some native blood in her."

"It may not be important. We judge people from their blood lines. That can be a mistake, sometimes. Many around us are now of mixed blood."

"He has wisdom."

He put the food in a plate. "What does he say to you?"

"He says that he sees the Creator all around us."

"What else?"

I ate the stew. "Christopher says that we must help others, even if it means sacrificing ourselves. This food is delicious."

"Eat, my brother." Tears rolled down his cheeks.

"What is wrong?"

"Nothing. I am happy. I understand now."

"Understand what?"

"The boy is a messenger. Next time you come back here, I will have a pen and paper. We must write his words down. The Great Spirit is revealing through him."

The Shaman walked in circles around his living room and chanted. Tears continued to roll down into the lines of his face. I didn't know what to make of it, but I enjoyed the warmth of the fire and lay down to sleep for a while.

I awoke after an hour or two; it was a good nap. I left Two-Moons under his blanket in his rocking chair, asleep in front of his hearth and went out into the snow that had fallen while I slept. I checked in on Christopher, who had still not fallen asleep. He was up because Marianna and Clint were arguing.

"I can stop whenever I want to," Clint shouted.

"Then why don't you? You're always drunk."

The shouting was causing Christopher anxiety.

"Christopher, I feel Clint's anger. I will spend the rest of the night between the Thunderbird rocks."

"I am glad you're here. I don't think Clint can control his anger."

"I am here for you."

I woke early and could tell that Christopher would not wander out. Marianna was up and making some breakfast; Clint had left the cabin and returned to his own home.

I moved quickly over to Hasselbeck's base camp. I wanted some information about how Rachel the skeptic was doing.

Hasselbeck was making coffee over a fire. Mongo walked out of the supply tent with a pan.

"You want some bacon?" Mongo asked.

Hasselbeck poked at the fire. "Sure."

"Wish Rachel were here. She'd love seeing this place with the little snow that fell during the night."

Hasselbeck poured Mongo a cup. "It's gonna be a while. Doctors say she'll be out of action for six months for the PT on that leg." He drank some coffee. "She still can't remember anything other than the bear attack."

Mongo cooked the bacon over the fire. "I found her tent and gear by Round Lake—right where she said it'd be. Bear destroyed everything. I found this." He tossed a small telephone to Hasselbeck. "Her cell phone lost GPS at 6:23 AM. That's when it was damaged in the attack."

"Hold it…. We got back here at, must have been 6:40. Give or take a few minutes."

"You got that map?"

Hasselbeck ran to his truck and pulled a map out. He rolled it out on the hood of his truck. "Show me the camp site that Rachael set up near Round Lake."

Mongo looked over the map. "It's right here."

"Mongo, that's three miles away, over rough terrain."

Mongo took a swig of coffee. "You're getting my point."

"Rachel couldn't have made it back here alone. Her leg was mangled."

"And she'd lost a lot of blood. There are few human beings who could cover that distance that quickly."

"Rachel couldn't do a five-minute mile before this happened. Most top athletes couldn't cover that distance in that time on a smooth track. There's no way that she could do this."

"It doesn't add up, Joey."

"Why can't she remember anything?"

"Dude, I know that I saw a big handprint on her back."

Hasselbeck looked at Mongo in astonishment. "And we have the door to Phil's car...."

"Ripped off and thrown forty feet away."

Hasselbeck walked around the truck and looked up to where the car door landed. He turned to Mongo. "Oh my God."

"I know. Dude, only a Squatch could do this."

Chapter Nineteen

I RESUMED MY NIGHT patrols of Deception Falls. Frankly, the town seemed to be a bit more peaceful these days. My surveillance program had reduced the number of drug dealers, gangsters, and women abusers. I was bored so I focused on the local political chatter, most of it driven by Vincent Zambelli.

He was making the rounds, stirring up trouble and asking for campaign contributions. He criticized Sheriff LaHood for being soft on crime and said that Mayor Wallace was accountable for that. He blamed them for all of the town's recent mayhem.

This was only one of the things that Zambelli was wrong about.

He met regularly with people who complained endlessly about their taxes. These people blamed others for costing them money.

"The state's eating into our income with these group homes."

"I think they should put the retarded people in big facilities the way they used to," Zambelli answered. "This shouldn't be our burden."

"These welfare cheats cost us a fortune."

"I will fight for regular people," Zambelli answered.

"The federal government takes too much. Why do we have to pay for programs for the Indians? Don't they have their own nation?"

Zambelli nodded. "They're another bunch ruining our way of life. And this mayor panders to these special interest groups."

So now the excuse to turn your back on others in need is to label them, "special interests." My loathing of these self-centered monsters was re-ignited. I wanted to crush Zambelli's skull.

It struck me as ironic that people complained about losing money but gave Zambelli money so he could replace Mayor Wallace. If you're low on cash, why give what little you have to him?

Money drove everything with these people. They viewed everybody who needed help as a burden. People like Christopher were lumped in with the native people and "welfare cheats", whoever they were. Zambelli had declared war on those weaker than him and many in the town joined his cause.

Money. It was all about money.

My people never thought to invent something like money. If someone in my domain needed something—a medicine plant, food, improved sleeping quarters—I got it for them. That was my obligation as the dominant one. And there is no bitching and moaning about it. The dominant one does his job and takes care of those he is responsible to. My father taught me that.

My people don't need money. They have Sasquatch.

The mayor treated his Native neighbors with respect. I heard him making phone calls to the Governor's office asking for money to help them move their village to higher ground because it had been flooded three times by coastal storms. It wasn't his town that was flooded, but he still took the time to help.

"It's from climate change," he told the governor's people. "We have to do something or these people will have nowhere to go."

Like my people.

After the initial trauma of the arrival of the people from the east, the Native people had managed to scratch out an existence on the margins of the dominant society. My people lived on the fringes of those living on the fringes.

Every now and then, a Native person would come into the deep woods to try to live off the land for a while. "It's a way of returning to the land and connecting to their ancestors," my father told me.

Two-Moons was such a person. As a young man, he went into the wilderness for two years and emerged a Shaman.

My father and I stalked Two-Moons for months, watching him from afar as he struggled to stay alive. We were astonished that he survived; he never sought shelter the way other humans do.

My father messaged me one day that the Shaman could sense our presence.

"How can he know of us?" I asked my father, through a mind-message.

"His mind has been opened through his suffering and sacrifice."

One evening, Two-Moons took off his shirt, painted his chest red with some clay and climbed a large boulder near the Lake of Souls. He placed fresh deer meat as an offering on the top of the rock, knelt down, and began chanting.

My father emerged from the darkness of the forest, silent, powerful, and dominant. He loomed over the shaman, holding his oak club.

"Smash his skull," I messaged. "No one will know. It's clear that his people aren't looking for him."

"No. He's a Shaman making an offering"

"He's a pain in the ass."

"We maintain a distant relationship with a select few. It has always been our way."

"Why?"

"Because our people are connected. He's come with an open heart, with respect. He has arrived at a critical moment in his vision quest."

"What does he want?"

"He seeks communion."

"But he is different from us."

"Not as different as you think."

My father swung the club over his head and let out a roar. *"WAHOOO!"* Then he swung the club at Two-Moon's head, stopping just before the club made contact.

Two-Moons never flinched.

"YAPAAH!" My father took the meat, placed some healing plants in front of Two-Moons and blended back into the woods.

I recall this story now as I watch Joseph Hasselbeck walking alone down a path toward the camp site where the brown bear attacked Rachel the skeptic. I've erected boundary markers to warn him. My kind erect wooden structures of large tree limbs twisted and wedged among each other to serve as a warning that you are not welcome here.

A wind storm didn't do this, Hasselbeck. It was I, Sasquatch.

I'm warning you, scientist. This is my domain. I will protect my people. I will kill you and anyone else who threatens our world.

I placed trees over the paths to block his access to the scene of the bear attack. My message is clear: turn around – you are not welcome here.

And still he comes. I notice that he isn't carrying a camera or any other technology. Hasselbeck has only brought a backpack.

He stops to examine another one of my wooden structures and shakes his head. "This wasn't caused by the wind or by a snow melt," he says aloud.

No, it wasn't. And you'd better realize that a creature that could twist heavy lumber in this manner can snap you in half and then go to lunch.

Turn around and leave. This is my domain.

He climbs over two more downed trees and steps into the clearing where Rachel's camp site had been. Hasselbeck scans the ground and the area around him. It is silent. Does he know that I am looming? Does he know that I can burst from the darkness and pound his body to a pulp?

Leave, Hasselbeck. I am weary of you. I should kill you now and end this. You are not someone who will be missed in your society. You're a fringe kook who has walked away from a normal human life to pursue a creature that most of your kind believes is a myth. And modern people no longer respect myths.

Don't you understand that you will destroy the reality - our reality - once you discover that the legend is just another kind of person?

Without myths, without magic, we are all just primates, scratching out an existence before we turn to dust. Once I am gone, once we are gone, the clock will begin ticking on your kind.

One day you will join us in the dust of time.

Hasselbeck reaches down and picks up the camera tripod from out of some weeds. I guess that nobody noticed it when they cleaned up the other day. He contemplates the tripod for a moment then whacks a pine tree with it. Whap! Whap! Then he opens his backpack and places a side of bacon on a rock. He looks up into the woods surrounding him.

"I know what you did for Rachel," he shouts. "And I know that you didn't have to do that."

This was getting interesting.

Hasselbeck looked into woods. "I have no idea how to express thanks to someone who's invisible. But I thought about something that a Shaman told me at a town meeting." He paused thoughtfully. "Maybe I can't find you with technology or with science. Maybe you're above our understanding. But that shouldn't mean that I don't show respect. I've brought you some bacon." He looked at the tripod, thoughtfully. "Thank you. My friend's life was worth the risk."

Chapter Twenty

JUST BEFORE DAWN, Christopher's humming stirred me from sleep. I peered over the edge of the snow-covered rock to see him walking toward me, flapping his hands and laughing.

"This must stop," I said. "You don't have feet like mine. Wear boots! You can't walk out into the snow in your bare feet. You'll freeze your toes off."

"You won't let that happen."

"What if I'm not here?"

He climbed onto my knee. "I always know when you are here." I held his feet in my fur-covered hands to warm them up. "You don't need boots or clothes. Your feet are like boots and you always have a coat of fur," he said. "You're proof of the Creator's wisdom."

"I'm over nine feet tall and weigh hundreds of pounds. I carry my own heat. You are not any of these things and can freeze out here."

"Sasquatch is the spirit of the forest, proof of the Creator's power."

"I am proof that he has a strange sense of humor." I

cleared some snow and lifted him onto the rock. "Why do you suppose he made us so different?"

He began drawing something with his fingers in the snow on top of the rock. "Love."

I blew on his tiny feet to warm them. "This I have to hear."

"Everything that is created is new and unique but loved by its creator. We look very different, but we are connected through time and blood."

"That is what my people say to each other. It helps us remember that we are not alone."

"In the beginning, there was only darkness. But the Creator wanted to fill the void, so He made the earth, the sky, the stars and the waters. That was love." Christopher drew an image of the earth and the sun in the snow. "The world was beautiful and it made Him smile. So, He opened his veins and poured some of his blood upon the earth, and life sprung from the ground. Trees grew and filled the forests, and grass filled the plains. Then He threw the earth, filled with the blood of life, into the sea and made fish and all the life that swims in the waters. Then He drew out some of the fish and gave them legs to crawl upon the land. They became all the animals that walk on the earth. This was love, too."

I looked at his drawings and smiled. "How did He create us?"

Christopher threw some snow into the air. "He took some of the earth and threw it to the stars, and created the birds of the sky. One of them was a giant bird who could bring rain to nourish the earth; the great bird could bring thunder too... The bird laid some eggs on a mountain. The first people were in those eggs. The eggs rolled down the mountain and the people emerged when the eggs cracked open. The Creator made people of different colors and sizes and furs. That is where we come from. We come from the stars and the Creator's love.

This is how we were created and why we are forever connected, even though we may look different."

I lifted the pine branches and showed him the image of the giant bird that was carved into the rocks that I slept under.

"There is the great bird. The people who are from here made that image thousands of years ago."

"Is your mother of the Native people?"

"I don't know."

"The Native people are very ancient."

"We are all very ancient. But each one of us is new. The earth is ancient, but every day is a new creation. Every person is a new creation, but people do not always see this."

I lifted him upon my shoulder. "Time for you to return to your cabin, little one."

"I know you worry about how humans act, but my mommy wouldn't shoot at you."

"Your mother is a good person. She is courageous. She will fight if she has to, but you're right, I don't think that she would shoot me."

"Last night, Clint hit her."

I pulled him down and sat him on a tree stump. "Tell me of this."

"Clint drank too much again. Mommy told him to stop or leave and then he hit her."

"I will snap his neck."

"He said he was sorry."

"I should still snap his neck. It will be a quick, painless death."

"Violence cannot be cured with violence."

"But we must protect your mother. She has protected others and has been kind to people in distress. I have seen this with my own eyes."

"I love my mommy. But I know that she will cry for Clint if you kill him."

I looked up at the sky seeking an answer. I didn't need all of these human entanglements. What was I doing with this human child?

I was the only person that he could talk to. He needed me.

I knelt down and put my hand on his shoulder. "A man never hits or intimidates a woman. Women are to be respected, always."

"Yes. And mommy accepted his apology."

I exhaled in frustration. "He must never do that again."

"I hope he won't."

"Me, too." We looked into each other's eyes. "All right, I will not kill him. But I don't understand why humans are unkind to each other, why they hurt each other, or why they deceive each other. It is beyond my understanding."

"People lose their way, but it doesn't mean that they can't change."

"I've never seen them change."

"We pay attention to the mistakes other people make, but never see our own faults. We are all imperfect. Have you ever met anyone who is without fault? Without sin?"

I rubbed my chin. "Only you, my little friend." I lifted him onto my back. "Christopher, I need to take a trip to see some relatives. It will take a few days."

"I will know when you have returned."

I paused. "And you will not wander in the woods?"

"I will not."

"The sun rises soon. Let's get you inside."

After I lifted Christopher through his window, I went deep into the forest and climbed to the top of a spruce that allowed me to see Mount Olympus in the distance. The snow-capped mountain was the domain of the great elder, Shattuck the Gray.

"I am coming, Shattuck."

"Do not climb the mountain. I have nothing to say to you."

"I seek your counsel."

"You will violate the boundaries of other dominant males. You know that we must maintain order to maintain our secrecy from the human world. You have no idea of the damage you can unleash by violating our laws."

"I must understand the meaning of this child's presence. He has entered our world for some reason."

"Do not violate the boundaries of the domains. You can unleash chaos."

"I must have your counsel. You know something I must learn."

"You will not like what you hear."

"I am coming nonetheless."

I climbed down and returned to the rear of the cabin to make sure that Clint left peacefully. Marianna walked him out to his car and kissed him good bye. I watched her as she watched him leave.

I considered flinging a rock through his car window and watching his brains splatter all over the interior of the car. But I had given my word to the boy.

Marianna held a mug of coffee that smelled wonderful. I could see that the peace of the woods in snow called to her. Marianna strolled down the path that leads to a parking area but paused to look at some birds on a tree branch. She smiled and drank a little more coffee then looked down.

"Oh my God!" she gasped.

Marianna saw one of my footprints in the snow.

Chapter Twenty-One

"AWESOME, RANGER CARINO!" Mongo exclaimed as Hasselbeck crouched down to photograph my foot prints.

Hidden behind a patch of thick bushes, I watched Hasselbeck and Mongo unloading their equipment.

"This is one of the biggest I've ever seen," Hasselbeck said. He looked up at Marianna and smiled. "This Big Foot is over nine feet tall. You're really lucky to have him visiting you."

Marianna held herself as though chilled. "I have a disabled kid to protect. I don't feel lucky."

Hasselbeck looked at her with concern. "We've never heard of a Squatch harming people."

But one made you shit in your tent, Hasselbeck. Get away from my people! We don't need your cameras and listening devices. I will leave dozens foot prints around your base camp if I have to. I'll throw rocks at your trucks to draw your attention away from here. Leave this family!

Mongo chomped on a donut. "They don't want interaction. They stay away from people."

"I believe that they've actually mastered avoiding

human interaction," Hasselbeck said calmly. "I'm betting that he was just passing through."

Marianna smiled. "Maybe it's just a big guy looking for a date."

"You got nine-foot-tall guys running barefoot in the snow after you?" Mongo said.

Hasselbeck smiled. "I bet you have guys chasing after you all the time. But look at the foot print—it's clearly not human."

Marianna shook her head. "It's got five toes and all that. How can you tell it's not human?"

Mongo took off one of his sneakers. "Check this out. You'll see." He put his bare foot in the snow.

Realization began to show on Marianna's face. "There's no arch...even the way the toes splay out...Oh my God."

"Welcome to the club, Ranger Carino," Mongo smiled. "You've got a Squatch living near you."

"I've tracked all sorts of animals—I'm a ranger. And I can tell you that this is no bear track either."

Hasselbeck put a ruler next to the print. "I have a theory that Big Foot evolved along-side us, watching us develop, observing our culture evolve, watching us multiply...." He photographed the print with a small camera. "...watching how we dominate the environment..." He looked down. "...and the way we treat our fellow man."

Marianna studied his face. "Go on."

"I think that these animals are another type of sentient primate. Maybe they reproduced at a slower rate and could never keep up with our population increases. We were out-competing them at every turn. So, at some point, they made a decision."

Marianna's blue eyes focused on his thoughtful expression. "A decision to do what?"

"To avoid us at all costs." Hasselbeck sighed. "Look at what is going on with the pipeline. Despite all we have learned from history about our treatment of native cultures, we're still willing to ram this thing through a sacred site because the dominant culture decides it's in their best interest. Can you blame the Big Foot species for shunning us? Even though they're super-intelligent, they chose not to have a culture based on objects, the way we do. A culture that makes things—art, pottery, buildings...."

"Roads, schools, even government," Mongo interrupted.

Hasselbeck smiled. "Institutions like museums and beautiful parks. And beautiful Park Rangers." Marianna smiled back. "Culture leaves a record of our humanity. Every object we make says 'man was here'." Hasselbeck crouched down to study the print again.

Marianna reflected on what Hasselbeck said. "What kind of culture would that leave them?"

"A culture of inter-connected consciousness," Hasselbeck looked up at the snow-covered forest canopy. "Look at how inter-connected everything is here. Just look at how that vine is weaved between the branches of that tree. Look at tangle of leaves there—it's actually a squirrel's nest. See how all living things rely on each other and become part of each other. Everything living is reliant on other living things." He turned to Marianna. "This is what they're like. They're all connected to each other on some basis that we don't understand. And they've never lost their connection to each other, the way we humans have. I believe that they communicate telepathically, on some basis."

"That's amazing," Marianna said.

"It's just a theory we are beginning to understand. To some Native Americans, the Sasquatch seem like spirits, transcendent beings that appear and disappear." Hasselbeck looked at Marianna. "Like Gods."

"You have to think about how the Native Americans view them in their myths," Mongo said. "Folk history often reflects real history. Oral traditions provide important clues."

"It's not just Native Americans," Hasselbeck said to Mongo. "Even Europeans have legends of Giants. Heck, the first story composed in Old English was *Beowulf*. There was his struggle with Grendel."

"Grendel was a Squatch," Mongo said confidently.

"Beowulf defeated Grendel and saved the Danes from his marauding. The Nordic Saga tells us that Grendel killed and ate dozens of warriors. That he was impervious to weapons and that no one could defeat him in battle. Until Beowulf suddenly appeared and saved them. Beowulf became Western Civilization's first action hero."

Marianna smiled. "Sort of like a super-hero?"

"Well, yeah. But I don't know. History is told by the winners," Hasselbeck looked a Marianna sadly. "It's told by those who could write. So, we're left with the story that Grendel was a monster. Maybe he was, maybe he wasn't. Maybe we've become the monsters. Maybe he was just one of these animals, and he became involved with humans when he shouldn't have." Hasselbeck looked around for more tracks.

I was worried that he would see Christopher's tracks *and* my tracks together. That would be a disaster. Good thing I carried him back to the cabin.

"Would you mind if we did some night work around your cabin?" Hasselbeck asked Marianna.

"I have a pretty complicated life," she sighed. "This is not really my property. The park service owns the cabin. The Superintendent of Parks lets me live here with my son."

"We'll respect your situation," Hasselbeck said. "Has your son mentioned anything about Big Foot? Sometimes kids are scared of something they've seen, but they're equally scared of talking about it."

"My son can't talk," Marianna said. "Christopher is disabled and non-verbal."

"Oh," Hasselbeck said. "I'm sorry."

"Don't be," Marianna said. "Christopher has gifts that no one but me really sees. He loves the woods. He becomes so calm, so peaceful in the forest. It's like, I don't know, like God talks to him here." She smiled at Hasselbeck. "If anyone could see God or a Big Foot, it would be Christopher."

Hasselbeck nodded. "Hey, tell you what, how about I bring you and Christopher some dinner this week? You pick the night. I'll come over and we'll just eat and talk. This way you can get to know me, and then you can decide whether we should do more work here."

Marianna looked at him. "Can I think about that?"

Hasselbeck smiled. "Please do. Here's my card."

They shook hands, smiling gently to each other.

I watched Hasselbeck and Mongo walk back to their truck.

"So, Joey," Mongo smiled, "is dinner part of our usual field work approach?"

"Shut up and get in the truck," Hasselbeck said with a smile. "She's the most beautiful, compelling woman I've ever met."

Great. Now is getting involved with Marianna. How damned complicated did my life need to be?

It was time to climb Olympus and seek the counsel of Shattuck the Gray, even if it meant crossing the domains of other dominant males.

Chapter Twenty-Two

"WHAT ARE YOU doing in my lands?" shouted the young dominant male as I ran through a field in his domain.

"Just passing through to visit the Gray One," I answer, blowing by him.

He runs alongside me, enraged. "You have no right to be here! Go back to your lands."

"I make no claims and will pass through and be gone. Same for the return trip."

"You're violating our boundaries. Upon my fathers' honor, I will destroy you for trespassing."

"Lighten up, fuzzy. I recall your father."

"What do you recall of him?" He grabs my shoulder.

I turn and kick him into a thicket of poison ivy. "Enough to know that you don't have half his balls. Be gone and stop worrying."

"Trespasser! You won't get past the next domain. My neighbor is larger than you and treacherous as well."

"Thank you for the information." I pick a smooth, palm-sized rock. "See you on the way back."

"Prepare yourself for the final swim in the Lake of Souls!"

Nice kid. He's got a bright future. I will have a woman send him some meat after the Elk migration.

Dominant males require territory. To keep the peace, boundaries are strictly enforced and respected by neighboring dominant males. The elders decided that we can't afford to lose males, who protect the others in their domains, so unnecessary border wars should be avoided whenever possible.

This is why crossing boundaries causes so much stress. My need to have my questions answered was also causing stress. I could feel the judgements of others in their mind-messages.

I could feel the weight of the criticism they did not directly communicate.

"How dare Sasquatch question Shattuck the Gray."

"Who is he to believe that he can question the way things are."

"He is a radical and a threat to us all."

Keeping a good pace, I cross into the domain of an established, powerful male. This next fellow is the real deal. He's just as tall as I am, and though I hear that he has some gray showing, he is indeed treacherous.

Age and treachery will defeat youth and strength. I need to be wary.

I cross the well-marked boundary—no missing this one's scent—and run full blast. "I am passing through to consult with Shattuck the Gray," I message him. "I seek no trouble."

"But found it you have!"

Out of the corner of my eye, I see him swing down from a giant pine, wielding oak. Had I not seen him at the last minute, my skull would have been crushed. As it was, he smacked my shoulder and I fell to the dirt in agony.

"Did you take me for a fool like the large adolescent next door?" He roared as he landed in front of me.

I rose to my feet, dusting the dirt off myself. "No, I didn't. But I haven't come here to fight you. I am traveling to seek the counsel of Shattuck."

He pointed at me with the club. "You will have to fight me to get it."

I charged him. "Then let's see if you can swing that club better this time, old goat!"

He took the bait and prepared to swing, giving me just enough time to load the throw. He didn't see the rock until it hit him square in the forehead. He fell to the floor, dazed but still conscious. I loomed over him. "You will recover in due time."

"*Ahh*, my vision is blurry!"

"You're lucky that you're seeing at all. Had I wanted you dead, you would be. Next time, attack from the sun to achieve greater surprise. Had you done so, you wouldn't be looking up at me with blurred vision." I knelt over him. "This wisdom I give you in exchange for safe passage on the way back. I have an appointment to keep."

Within a few hours, an icy river at the base of Mount Olympus flowed before me as I fashioned a club out of heavy oak.

Shattuck messaged me. "I told you not to come. I have nothing to say to you."

"Yes, you do old one. Respectfully, there are things that you haven't told me."

"Let the wolves give you counsel."

I turned to see that a pack of wolves had surrounded me. Shattuck was always good at communicating with predators. He taught this skill to me.

They circled, probing for a moment of weakness. The hair on their backs arched as they growled and bared their teeth. I slowly moved away from the rocky shore line toward a patch of smooth sand. The wolves followed. I raised the club over my head.

"Which of you chooses to die first?"

The lead male leapt at my throat and missed, falling to the ground. I clubbed him across the back and he fell away yelping.

Another attempted a jump as I beat him aside with a devastating swing. One grabbed my other arm and bit into my flesh. I flung him far out into the river where the current took him away. My blood dripped onto the sand as another lunged and bit my leg. My club smacked his jaw and he ran away down the river bank.

One grey-eyed male remained. We stood glaring at each other. He turned and jumped onto a boulder. *"WU-UH-WOOO,"* he howled.

"WAAAHAH!" I returned.

Then he was gone. I pressed river mud against my wounds and rested briefly against the boulder. A few minutes later, I waded into the cold river and submerged myself. It was important to bathe, to purify your heart, before visiting an elder. It is our way.

I ascended Mount Olympus and eventually got to the edge of the tree line. Nothing but rock and snow and ice. However, I wanted to make sure that Shattuck and his guards knew that I was near, so I whacked a pine tree three times.

After another two hours of strenuous climbing, I stood at the entrance of the Gray One's cave.

"I am here, wise one."

Two large males burst from the cave, swinging clubs. "This is where you die, you insolent heretic!" one of them screamed.

I stood my ground. "Perhaps so, but I will take you with me to the grave if I am not allowed to see the Grey One."

"We will make you dig your own hole and then we will stuff you in it," the other growled.

I grinned as I raised my club. "Then I will dig one for you as well."

He lunged and I countered his swing by shifting my position. The second attacker had to get around the one I was dueling. The sound of our war howls and our clubs smacking against each other echoed down the mountain. One scored a hit on my back a moment before my strike to his thigh leveled him. I engaged the other and began driving him up toward the cavern.

"Enough!" Shattuck shouted. He stood at the entrance of his cave, his long white fur whipped about him in the wind. His red eyes burned into me. "You've earned your counseling session. Let him pass."

Chapter Twenty-Three

I FOLLOWED THE ELDER deep into his cave, the two angry, wounded escorts following behind.

"I see that you bathed," Shattuck grunted. "For someone so willing to risk the discovery of our people, you have followed traditions quite well."

"I seek only your wisdom, great one."

Shattuck turned and smacked me with the back of his hand. Even at one hundred and thirty-seven years old, he still had enormous strength. I rolled on the floor, barely conscious.

"You are arrogant!"

I shook my head. "I seek the truth with peace in my heart."

"So you say. I've seen your kind before. Experience some loss and suffering and you feel the world owes you an explanation. You need to find the meaning in it all." He pulled me up by the hair on the crown of my head. "The world doesn't owe you anything." He held my face in his hands and looked into my eyes. "Life and death are their own explanations. When you have lived as long as I, you will see this. Maybe then you will have the right to seek truth."

"Forgive me," I mumbled.

"Arrogance negates humility!"

I noticed a human skull laying on the ground. "What is that doing here?" I asked.

"That is not your concern! That stupid human wandered in here years ago. He made a mistake in coming here, just like you. You seek the truth, you say. Why?"

"I need to understand the human boy-child who can mind-speak."

"Nonsense."

"It's true."

"I don't see how. Sit." I sat on the floor in front of a small fire. "Eat."

An escort gave me some dried meat. "The only humans who could come close to such a skill have been pushed to the brink of extinction, like us. To a handful of Native ones, we are known only as *spirits*." Shattuck ate some meat as well. The old bastard still had good teeth. "The modern people are mindless, so we must remain invisible to them. We shall continue in the shadows. Someday they may exterminate each other and we may be able to walk in the sun without looking over our shoulders. But until then, man is to be shunned."

"What if that is not the path we are meant to walk?"

"You don't even know the path you're on. You can't know your destiny because you don't know your past."

"I need to know."

"Wrong! You *want* to know. You're more like the humans every day, confusing what you want with what you need. You're confused because you're spending too much time around them." Shattuck paused. "Hand me that skull."

I reached over, picked up the skull and handed it him.

"Do you really think that I stay here on the mountain just because the color of my fur helps me to blend in with the snow and ice? Do you believe it is because I can communicate with the other Elders on other mountains far away? Is it so that when you look up at the mountain, you know that we will always rule from above?" He examined the skull. "No. It's because, from the top of Mount Olympus, all things are clearer. I have seen males more dominant than you lost to winds of time. In the end, even the most powerful are left to the dust." He crushed the skull with his hand. The broken pieces crumbled onto the cave floor. "You think you know the humans."

"I want to understand *this* boy and what is happening around us."

Shattuck shook his head. "You know nothing. Their chaotic nature is starting to rub off on you. Shun them! That is my counsel. You've heard what you need to hear."

"Something is changing. I can feel the Thunderbird stirring."

Shattuck glared at me. "What do you know of the God of the Sky?" He pulled on the long grey beard that hung from his chin, considering my statement. "He stirs because the humans are desecrating their world. Someday soon, they may well destroy themselves."

"What if they destroy us as well?"

"That is what we must avoid. That is why we shun them. They are toxic to us."

"They're incompetent, small and weak."

"No!" he roared. "They are cunning and devious." He gritted his teeth. "They can spin lies into powerful illusions. They use their words to twist truth so that truth is lost." He spit into the fire. "What we can conceal with a touch of our hands, they conceal with words. We evolved to share consciousness; they evolved to deceive each other. They make our kind insane."

"How do you know of this? Our encounters are so rare."

He glared at me and sneered. "As well they should be."

"The boy is different."

"In what way?"

"He is open and sincere. The Creator speaks to and through him."

"So *you* say. I have stalked the shadows for over a century. I have never encountered such a human."

"He is different. Even the Shaman says so."

He poked at the fire with a club. "You're prepared to risk the revelation of our existence for this child? Are you insane?" He raised his club. "I should kill you now and be done with this drama." The escorts moved forward, growling. Shattuck raised his hand. "Leave us!" They faded into the darkness of the cave, growling. "Look into the fire." He retrieved an old jug, opened it and sprinkled some liquid onto the stones around the fire. The rocks hissed and smoke rose from the hearth. "Breathe in and look into the smoke."

The smoke billowed into the darkness of the cave. "I am freeing memories from our past. This will take all my strength." The smoke rose. "There was a time when we lived in a cautious peace with the Native humans. We gave each other gifts of food and beautiful objects, like this jug. We brought salmon for their celebrations. Twice a year, they offered sacrifices and held ceremonies to honor us." Images of the Native ones in ceremonial dress appeared in the smoke. They were dancing around a large fire. "They sang our praises. They called us by our name—C'iatqo—Immortal Spirit Guardian of the Dark Woods. They worshiped us as Gods. Then *they* came...." Slowly, images of horse drawn carriages rolling into a lush valley appeared. "I was young then. I saw the White ones come into the valley for the first time through the Deception Pass. My father, brothers, and all of our clan were astonished. 'What kind of people could build such things?' we wondered. We marveled at their wagons." Shattuck threw more liquid onto the rocks and more smoke rose into the gloom. "And then we saw our brothers, the Native ones ride out to greet the Whites. The chief of the Quinalt of the Skokum River, Wise-Bear, they called him, led his warriors toward them. He raised his arms to greet them. He wanted to know their intentions." He drank from the jug and spat the liquid into the fire, which flared violently. "Then it happened."

In the smoke, I saw one of the Whites draw a rifle and shoot the chief. Then gun fire blasted from the other covered wagons. "When the Skokum tried to flee, the White men shot them in the back. They killed them all. Then they scalped them and celebrated."

The images of the slaughter were repulsive. I held my stomach, feeling nauseous.

"I see horror."

"Yes, but there is more. What the Whites did was horrible. What we did was worse. That night we raided their camp." Shattuck looked into the fire.

"We did?"

"We brought our oak. There were dozens of us." He closed his eyes and a far-away sadness shook him. "Silently we moved, like demons in the night. We waited until they slept. Then we launched our attack. Merciless were we." Shattuck looked at me coldly. "We killed them all. We bashed their skulls in and ripped their organs out. Their women, their children, even their infants. All of them."

"We did this?"

"It is even worse. Horror begets horror. Other Whites assumed that it was the Native humans who committed this atrocity. Our blood lust was repaid with the lives of thousands of Native ones. They were blamed for our sins and paid a dreadful price. They were hunted and enslaved. Their culture was obliterated. Many died from disease and despair over the world they had lost."

I buried my face in my hands. "I did not know."

"Because we did not tell you. I am the last of those who were there. When I die, I shall take my sins with me and I will suffer for them. This is why I tell you, *beware of man*. Unless you shun him, he will drag you into hell. He will steal your soul. This is why you must leave the boy. Nothing good can come of this. We must maintain our secrecy, no matter what the cost. You risk losing our world the way our brothers lost theirs. Shun this boy."

"But he can mind speak."

"And this means what? You have said that his own kind cannot hear his words."

"Two-Moons feels that he is a messenger."

Shattuck glared at me. "Have you touched his hands?

"Yes. Why?"

"What did you feel?"

"Energy—a vibration. I'm not sure."

"Give me your hands."

"What are you doing?"

"I must feel the imprint of his mind within you. I must know why he is this way—if what you say is true." With one hand he gripped my hand; he placed his other hand on my forehead. "Why can he speak only to you? *Harrgh. Harrgh*," he groaned. We fell onto the floor of the cave, locked in a trance. The jug fell over, pouring liquid into the fire. Smoke engulfed us in the darkening cave.

In the smoke I saw terrifying images of men in white coats, like the ones who supervised Tang. They poked me with needles and held machines that shined light into my eyes. Everything was cold and stark and white. They placed me in a giant tube while hammers pounded the walls. I was being tortured. Shattuck and I howled in horror. What were these demons?

Then they were torturing the boy. The men in white coats harmed Christopher so that his mind was altered. And I couldn't stop them. Marianna couldn't stop them. Her blue eyes burned into me.

"My son! They've destroyed my son. Bring him back to me."

All I could do was watch.

I awoke to see Shattuck lying on the floor, moaning. "Wise one, what did you see?"

His eyes opened. "Hell. The modern ones are even more horrible than their ancestors. What they seek to do to you is horrible. What they did to this child is unspeakable!" Shattuck vomited his meat onto the cave floor. "The flames. The flames!"

"What have they done to Christopher?"

He covered his eyes. "Shun him! Shun the humans!"

"I must know!"

"Shun him!"

I shook him. "Tell me!" The guards rushed, clubs drawn.

"No!" he shouted at them. They retreated back into the blackness once again, growling. "They poisoned him. They sacrificed him. And I don't know why."

"They sacrificed the child?! Their own religion says they can't do that. Their God would stop them!"

"Their God did not. The vision is true."

"What kind of monsters would do that to a child?"

Hate burned in his eyes. "We should kill them all."

We lay on the floor, exhausted from our visions, drained of emotion. A dark, dreamless sleep fell upon me.

Shattuck woke me with a shake early the next morning. "Head to the tree line before sunrise, this way no humans will see you against the snow and rock. You're not gray, like me—yet." He handed me some dried meat. "You must not tell others what I've told you."

"I won't."

"Good." He looked into the smoldering embers. "I have a request."

"What do you need?"

"When I die, do not take me to the Lake of Souls. Burn my body and scatter my ashes to the wind." Shattuck turned and walked into the darkness.

I left the cave, exhausted. As I walked down the mountain, I saw lights far away in a valley along a river. It was one of the settlements that Shattuck had told me about, glowing like a swath of stars in the pre-dawn night. It was stunning.

"They are like the stars," I thought.

How could people build something so beautiful and yet wreck a child?

How could we have a future when we held such dark secrets of the past?

I sought the counsel of Shattuck for wisdom and truth. What I learned disgusted me. Shattuck was full of rage and self-loathing. I finally understood him.

That was when I realized the cost of secrets. The horror that Shattuck spoke of had cast darkness over my people. The price for maintaining secrecy was that we would forever live in the shadows. And now I knew what the rabbi was talking about.

We are Cain.

Chapter Twenty-Four

AS I DESCENDED the mountain, I knew that I would have to let go of Christopher. Our kind just wasn't meant to integrate. We were too different and too trapped within the sins committed by our ancestors. Shattuck was right: our species needed to separate from each other lest we trigger a disaster that we couldn't control. Our history had proven that.

But how could I walk away from this child when I was the only person he could speak to? His own culture had poisoned and sacrificed him for reasons that were beyond my understanding. Whatever the reasons, the abuse he suffered as an infant triggered a cascade of problems for Christopher and his mother that lead them to be outsiders among their own people. Like us, they were driven into the shadows, shunned and rejected.

Where was justice for this child?

As I rose from the icy river, I looked up to the sky. "Why have you brought me to this end?" I asked the creator. "What is the purpose of these experiences?"

I walked back through the other domains, unchallenged, in silence.

I approached the ranger's cabin just after sundown to begin the necessary but painful process of separation that I knew must begin. It was best for Christopher and best for me. Yet my heart was heavy.

It was time to vanish forever, deep into the woods of my domain.

Then I heard the gun fire.

"I'm gonna shoot a Big Foot!" Clint shouted after discharging another round as he staggered down the path behind the cabin.

"Christopher," I messaged. "What is Clint doing?"

"Sasquatch, stay away, Clint is drunk and he's shooting mommy's gun."

"Where is your mother? Are you safe?"

"I'm in my room on the floor. Mommy went to a meeting at the town hall about the group home. She asked Clint to watch me, but he became angry and started drinking after he played a message on the phone machine from the Big Foot researchers. They're coming later this week."

Another round went off. "Don't need no researchers messin' with my woman!" Clint shouted. "God damned Big Foot!"

"Clint started drinking. He's angry and jealous."

"He's bat-shit crazy beyond all reason and I've had enough of him."

"What are you going to do?"

A round blasted into a pine tree, three feet to my right. "I'm going to pulverize his skull until his eyes pop out of their sockets!"

"No! Violence does not cure violence."

"But it can stop it. He's a menace! He's risking your life and mine, betraying your mother's trust."

"You must find another way."

"It's very difficult to consider creative options when someone's shooting at you."

"Die, you fat, hairy baboon!" Clint shouted before firing another round in the direction of the cabin.

"Are you hit? That bullet struck the cabin."

"I think it hit the roof. I'm fine."

"You're never fine when someone's shooting at you. How did he know that I was back?"

"He doesn't know. He's drunk and he wants to prove that my mommy doesn't need the researchers, that he is all she needs."

"He's insane."

"Clint threatens mommy every time she does something without him, even when she just talks to another man."

"I'm the man!" Clint yelled with bravado. "We don't need outsiders to come here and deal with this. I'm the man. I handle it."

"Let's see how he handles it when I rip his arms off."

"Then he will be left armless but still angry."

"You ask too much, Christopher. This maniac needs a killing."

"You must find another way. The creator asks this of us."

Oh, damn it to hell.

I moved silently behind some brush and allowed Clint to storm past me on the trail.

"Whooup! Whooup!"

Clint turned with alarm. "What the heck is that?"

I threw a rock and hit him in the ass.

He danced around in pain. "Ahh! Who threw that at me?"

"AHWOOOO!"

"That's it, Big Foot. You're dead now!" He fired two more rounds that missed the tree I was hiding behind. He walked toward my hiding place, gun at the ready. "I'm gonna kill you now, you hairy mother...."

I bolted from behind the tree and ran right at him, growling.

"Holy shit!"

I slammed his torso with my elbow and sent him sprawling up the path. He staggered to his feet and shot another round at the place where he thought I would be standing.

But I had already moved on to a new attack point. I ran at him again from the other direction and rammed him from behind. Clint was propelled through the air and came crashing down into a muddy patch of wet leaves. The gun landed somewhere beyond his reach on the dark forest floor.

"Help me! Help! I'm being attacked by Big Foot!" He swiped mud and leaves off his face and looked up to see me towering over him.

"It is you who attacked me!" I grabbed him by his throat and lifted him off the ground. "You've brought violence and pain to my people. I should crack your rib cage open and rip your lungs out."

"Aghh!" Clint's eyes were wide open in terror and shock. "Oh God. You're real!"

"I'm as real as it gets, you abusive bastard."

"You're going to kill me!"

"Not on this day. I've been advised that the Creator wants us to resolve problems without violence."

"What?!"

"I have different plan for you." I placed my other hand on his forehead. A moment later, he blacked out.

I climbed down from the pine tree a short time later. "Christopher, he is secure. Clint will no longer be a threat to you."

"What did you do to him?"

"I gave him an opportunity to reconsider his negative attitudes."

"He still has all of his arms and legs?"

"He does. But it's his mind that causes him problems. He's resting comfortably for now and when he wakes, he will remember nothing of our meeting."

"I am glad that you did not kill him. Will he sleep until mommy comes home? He is so angry."

"He may not be any less angry, but it will not matter. You will be safe."

"Why?"

"Because Clint will need some help. He's hanging by his belt from a sturdy branch, forty feet above the trail. Did you say that the meeting on the group home was at the town hall?"

Chapter Twenty-Five

MY APPROACH TO the old town hall had to be stealthy. LaHood had his deputies on guard in front to set the no-nonsense tone. The place was packed with humans, some carrying signs of protest about the plan to open another group home for disabled people, some carrying signs in support.

Gazing through the windows I could see Vincent Zambelli sitting the front row, surrounded by his supporters. They carried posters that read, *No More Group Homes— Taxed Out of Ours* and *Special Needs = Special Interests*.

Marianna sat across the aisle from these protesters with a small group of people who I gathered opposed Zambelli and his rabble.

Mayor Wallace and town trustees sat in front at an elevated table, the same way Hasselbeck and his researchers had a few months before. I could see LaHood standing in the back of the room, arms folded, eyes fixed on Zambelli.

The tension between the two men caused them to glare at each other.

"That finishes off the regular business of the Deception Falls Town Board. We're going to commence the public hearing on the proposed group home for the disabled, located on Salmon Run Road," the mayor said. "Now let me be absolutely clear, we're going to let everyone speak. I don't care if we're here 'til midnight. We're all going to be respectful of each other's opinions. We're all going to act like good citizens."

Oh, I disagree, Your Honor. Good citizens wouldn't whine and complain about taking care of each other. Good citizens wouldn't moan about their community being "over-saturated" with the disabled. Good citizens would listen to their priests and rabbis and do what has to be done to help their neighbors.

Good citizens wouldn't exterminate native people or hunt other beings to the point of extinction.

I had half a mind to set the old wooden structure ablaze and dance in the parking lot as they all roasted to death. But then I wouldn't be able to look Christopher in the eye. And besides, Marianna was in there.

The first few speakers were with Zambelli; they opposed the group home because of the cost. Zambelli stood and repeated the opinion that the community was "over saturated" with the disabled.

"What does that mean?" Wallace asked.

"Well, this would be the third group home in our town. We only have eight thousand people living in Deception Falls."

"So, are you aware of some formula that determines "saturation"? We'd have a total of twenty-two people living in these homes. Twenty-two people would be *saturating* eight thousand? What do you mean?"

"You're caving into the state; these homes are hurting our tax base and property values."

The room burst into cheers and chants of *Zambelli for Mayor! Zambelli for Mayor!*

No one noticed Whale-Shit escorting Two-Moons into a seat at the back of the room.

The next speaker came from Marianna's group. "My name is Amy Dachel, Fourteen Hoh Street. I've lived in this town for over forty years and I've taught our children at the Tioga Grammar School for twenty-seven of those years. I find the tone of some of my fellow citizens disappointing. Have any of you looked around? We have all sorts of children and adolescents with health problems.

"You're being an alarmist, lady," Zambelli said aloud.

"Order," shouted the mayor, using his gavel for emphasis.

"Think about who's living in these homes that you're protesting against," Dachel added. "It might be your kids someday."

"We raise our kids right!" somebody shouted.

"The homes are costing us a fortune!" another called out.

The mayor banged the gavel again. "Order!"

"These homes might be for our children one day," Dachel responded. "I don't care what they cost. It doesn't matter what they cost."

I wanted to give this teacher some fresh meat. She was a strong woman.

Zambelli was recognized and he took to the podium to cheers and the chants of *Zambelli for Mayor!* He raised his hands and his crew immediately quieted down. "I am Vincent Zambelli, twenty-seven Willow Brook Road."

I knew where that was.

"I moved here a few years ago because I loved this part of the country, because the people were self-reliant and because they were fiercely independent—the way real Americans should be." His supporters rose and applauded. "Back east, where I come from..."

"New Jersey," the mayor interrupted.

"Are you going to interrupt me? I have the podium."

"He's just pointing out that you don't come from Kansas," LaHood barked from the back of the room. The people around Marianna burst into laughter. The mayor frowned at LaHood.

"Where I came from," Zambelli continued, "government became hostage to special interests. They used regulations and government mandates to push regular, hard-working people around. Government became a bully and an ogre...."

Now that I know where you live, I'll show you a real ogre, Zambelli.

"This mayor and this board are caving into the plans of the state. Where does this stop?" His supporters again rose in support, cheering.

Mayor Wallace banged the gavel harder this time. "Order please!"

"Why isn't the state picking up the cost of the hit to our tax base?" Zambelli demanded loudly. "Why aren't you fighting this, Mr. Mayor? Why are you selling our town down the river?" More applause erupted. "I hope that you vote *no* and refuse a town permit for this group home!"

"Our legal counsel advises that very few local decisions are ever upheld, Mr. Zambelli," Wallace answered. "Do you want us to waste your tax dollars on legal fees?"

"I want you to fight for the town. If you won't, then we need a mayor who will!" Zambelli walked away from the podium and was awarded high-fives and pats on the back by his supporters. I could see that the mayor was red-faced and humiliated.

No one noticed as Marianna quietly walked to the podium.

"My name is Marianna Carino. I live with my son, Christopher, in the Ranger Cabin in Cascadia Park."

"You're living at tax payer expense," someone shouted.

"I pay rent to the Park Service," she said calmly. "May I speak?"

"You're not even a town resident!" Zambelli said aloud.

LaHood walked down the side aisle. "Shut your pie hole, Vincent. The lady lives in an unincorporated part of the town. She has a right to be heard."

The mayor looked at the other board members who shrugged. "Go ahead Miss Carino."

"I have a son who can't speak, so I have to speak for him. He's a gentle soul who wouldn't hurt anyone. Christopher sees the world differently than we do. When he is in a bustling town or a busy school room, he gets confused. I can feel his anxiety. But when he's home and sees the sky and the woods, he becomes filled with peace. This is what I want for my son—a peaceful, meaningful life in a community that loves him and will look after him." Marianna's eyes misted. "I ask all of you to think about this for two reasons. First, because my son is your son and second, I won't live forever.

"When he was an infant, I took Christopher for a well-baby visit. The pediatrician and the nurses smiled as they gave him his shots. A few hours later, he had seizures. During the days that followed, he had more and more seizures. Christopher was never the same after he was given those vaccinations. My baby boy was gone. I asked if it was the shots they gave him that got him so sick, but none of the doctors would affirm that. They just sent us from one specialist to the next to try to help Christopher. Finally, we were left with a label. They called him *autistic*. That was all."

"We've been on the road ever since, trying to find the right community in which to live comfortably and be accepted." Marianna looked down, paused, and turned to the crowd. "I'm weary of wandering. Someday Christopher will need a peaceful place to live and it will be up to all of you to take care of him; we like it here. We're not going to move anymore. This is our home. So, if you're not going to do it, you'd better think carefully: what happened to my child could've happened to yours." She turned back to the board. "Mayor Wallace, members of the board, please vote yes and let these people live here in peace."

The room fell silent as Marianna went back to her seat. LaHood stood at attention and nodded to her as she took her seat.

Two-Moons ambled down the center aisle with his oak cane, Whale-Shit in tow.

"Hello my old friend," the mayor said. "People, this is Two-Moons, Shaman of the Red Cedar Tribe—our neighbors from Tahola. Please tell us what you think, Two-Moons."

Two-Moons turned and looked at Zambelli's group, nodding. They all looked down. "It's not easy to look upon your neighbors with hard hearts, especially when one speaks with such dignity." He pointed toward Marianna. "You should hear this woman's words. Listen to what she is saying. Let her words move you. She is giving you a chance to atone and get right with the world. Instead of worrying about your taxes and property values, you should think of your souls. Think of what you can do for others. In the end, we are all returned to the Creator and to the dust of time. What you do with your life is important. Listen to what this woman has said." He faced the Mayor, "Hiyuma'si."

The mayor nodded.

Two-Moons turned and walked up the aisle, then paused by Marianna's chair. "You're Christopher's mother." He held out his hand and Marianna took it.

"Yes, I am."

"You are blessed to have such a son."

"You know my son?"

"Yes. I have a friend who keeps an eye out for him."

Chapter Twenty-Six

"SO, YOU LEFT him with your son and you come home from a meeting and..."

Marianna rolled her eyes. "You and I were at the same meeting, Sheriff."

"I know that very well, Miss Carino," LaHood smiled appreciatively. "Incidentally, Zambelli announced he's runnin' for Mayor after you left."

"He's despicable."

"I'll put in my papers if he's elected. Man's got no soul. Help me get the time line right...you come home and you hear Prince Charming screaming. You find him danglin' up there in the tree."

"Yes. Thank God for the volunteer firemen, otherwise he'd still be up there."

"It would have been fine with me if they just cut the branch and let 'im drop the forty feet."

As I watched from the woods, I found myself agreeing with LaHood. I was actually starting to like him.

"Well, he was drunker than a skunk and now I can't find my gun. I'm going to have to explain all this to my superiors. I asked him to take care of my son so I could go to the Town Hall tonight and I came back to this." Tears welled up in her eyes. "So, I cut *my* branch with him. I told him not to come back. Enough is enough."

LaHood looked up from his notepad. "Marianna, you're a fine woman and there are a lot of good men around our town. You don't need to settle."

She smiled. "Thank you."

"After he's released from the ER, I'm gonna ask that creep what he was doin' in the woods when he was supposed to be watching your son. Did he say how he got up that tree or how he ended up danglin' by his own belt strap?"

"He went on that I didn't need to talk to Doctor Hasselbeck and his researchers and that he went out to deal with the Big Foot himself."

"So, this idiot went out here lookin' to shoot a Squatch? Okay. That's about as logical as going fishing for the Loch Ness Monster. Add alcohol to an idiot's diet and anythin' goes." He swept the tree branch with his flashlight. "How the hell did our crazy Big Foot hunter get up there?"

"Maybe a Big Foot put him there," Hasselbeck interrupted. "I was at Lucy's Coffee Shop when I overheard one of your deputies talking about what happened, so I ran up here."

Marianna smiled. "Thanks for coming."

Yeah. Thanks, Hasselbeck. Keep following me and you'll be dangling upside-down from the same branch.

"You sayin' that a Big Foot put old Clint up there? Okay assuming that such a critter exists, why?"

Hasselbeck ignored LaHood's displeasure. "I'm not sure. There is so much that we don't understand about Big Foot."

That's right, Hasselbeck. You don't know anything about us. Go back to your tent and leave me and my kind alone.

Hasselbeck looked up at the branch. "This is amazing. Could Clint really have climbed that tree?"

"He worked in the tree removal business before he got fired last year. I guess he can climb."

"Okay." Hasselbeck scratched his chin. "How was he held up there?" It was clear he hadn't heard all the details.

Marianna giggled. "He was hanging by his belt."

"How did he manage that?" Hasselbeck asked.

"Yeah," LaHood followed. "What'd he say 'bout it, Marianna?"

"He said that he couldn't remember."

"Really?" Hasselbeck asked with rising curiosity.

"Numb-nuts heard your voice-mail message—you've made him really jealous. He got plastered and came out here to kill Big Foot."

Marianna looked up at the branch. "I could picture him, all full of bravado. He took my gun and seems to have fired it; some campers at Grind Creek heard shots. Then *boom*! He can't recall anything. Dumb fool."

Hasselbeck put his hand on Marianna's shoulder. "A few months ago, one of my team members was attacked by a brown bear on the other side of the park. Her leg was mauled and she almost died."

"I know," she said. "I saw the report. Tried to track the bear but couldn't find it."

"Somehow, she made it three miles back to the camp in world-record time on one leg, suffering massive blood loss. She can't remember how she did that, even though she vividly recalls the bear attack."

LaHood frowned. "So, you're tellin' me that these animals, the ones that no one has even proved exist, somehow induce amnesia in people?"

"I know that sounds crazy, but think of all the odd defenses that animals have evolved over the years. Chameleons have skin pigments that allow them to blend into the environment around them. There are frogs that secrete poisons."

"Yeah, but you're talking about some half-assed American mountain gorilla here."

Watch who you're calling a Gorilla, LaHood. I know where you park your car.

"Sheriff, these animals do everything they can to avoid people. One can imagine that they've developed quite a bag of tricks to remain off our radar."

LaHood frowned. "Yeah, but assuming this is true—and you're askin' me to accept an awful lot of strange stuff here—this Big Foot isn't really avoiding people. You'd be sayin' that Clint went out huntin' a Squatch in the back yard here and damn near got one."

"How did Clint end up on that branch, Sheriff?" Hasselbeck challenged.

"And you're sayin' one rescued your co-worker from a bear attack? Why would this animal do that?"

"I don't know," Hasselbeck said.

LaHood frowned. "Come on now, Dr. Hasselbeck, where's the evidence? One would think that we'd have a capture by now. I've been hearin' Squatch stories 'round these parts for forty years. I get that these lands support big predators, but an eight-foot primate? Come on."

"Parts of Olympic National Park haven't been visited by people in years," Marianna added. "There's a lot of land out there."

LaHood wasn't buying it. "But we'd have real evidence by now. Somethin' that big leaves bones and such."

"I think that they bury their dead," Hasselbeck said.

LaHood raised his eye brows. "You mean like people do? They go to church, too?"

Well, sort of. At least I listen to your priests and rabbis better than your own people do.

"We know that Neanderthals buried their dead and performed rituals. Their graves prove that. We're not the only creatures to have wondered about life and death."

LaHood rubbed his chin. "So Big Foot believes in a higher power?"

Hasselbeck's eyes focused on LaHood. "Maybe."

"Well maybe I'll invite him to our AA Meeting tomorrow night. He can make the coffee."

Hasselbeck directed his flashlight on the forest floor. "Mind if I look for more tracks?"

LaHood aimed his light on the floor as well. "Hey, there's a bullet casing here." He picked it up and held it under the light. "This is your department issue. We can charge numb nuts with discharging a fire arm recklessly." Both men began searching the forest floor in earnest.

"A lot of boot prints from the firemen," Hasselbeck said. "The whole area's been trampled."

LaHood pointed at a muddy patch of leaves. "Looks like a man fell in the mud here. Here's where he used his hand to get back up."

"That looks to be about the size of Clint's hand," Marianna said.

LaHood examined the hand print. "Well, it looks like your ex wasn't havin' any fun out here. I'm thinking he got his ass kicked."

"It's about time he got some of what he gives," Marianna said quietly.

Hasselbeck touched Marianna's hand. "I'm sorry."

"I'll be damned!" LaHood shouted. "I found your gun, Ranger Carino."

"Thank God," she answered.

LaHood looked at Hasselbeck in astonishment. "It's right here—in the middle of this enormous foot print."

Chapter Twenty-Seven

A FEW NIGHTS later, Vincent Zambelli was wrapping up his *I'm Running for Mayor Party* in the living room of his home on Willow Brook Road. I could see his petite wife scurrying around clearing drinks from the serving table and dumping uneaten food in the garbage.

"You're gonna be a great mayor," a pudgy male said. "This penne-al la vodka is delicious. This town needs new blood."

"Well, thanks," Zambelli grinned. "I appreciate your support."

"Mayor Wallace is a nice guy and all that. He's just not getting it done. The town's stuck in the mud."

"There hasn't been 'nough of a focus on the business district," another, taller male said while stirring his drink. "We at the Chamber of Commerce think it's time for a change."

"The guy spends too much time trying to please the tribes in the area," said the pudgy one. "I heard he's got some Native blood in him."

"Is that true?" Zambelli asked. "He doesn't have a Native American name."

"Most of the people in the area's tribes don't either,"

the tall man said. "We've all been mixed together around here. You know that Jack LaHood's part Quinault."

"I didn't know that," Zambelli said. "We need new blood running the Sheriff's department, too. Taking care of that will be a priority when I get in. I also want to shut down those group homes. Keep those houses on the tax rolls and begin lowering everyone's tax burden. They'll spend more money in town if they've got more in their pockets."

"That's what we want to hear," the pudgy man said with an air of triumph.

So, I guess that the mayor wasn't good for business and Zambelli, despicable though he be, would bring in more money. It was always about money.

Zambelli has his wife take a photograph of him standing next to the men. They all had big toothy grins.

I wanted to burst into the party and cram food down their throats until they choked—greedy, obnoxious, un-feeling bastards. I wanted to stuff the pudgy one into Mrs. Zambelli's trash compactor while everyone screamed in horror.

However, Zambelli was my target. I had very specific plans for him. I waited behind some trees in his back yard until everyone left. Then I moved to hide behind his backyard shed, near the garbage cans.

Men always take out the garbage. Zambelli would soon be mine.

Sure enough, Zambelli walked across the yard and placed bags of garbage into the cans. He placed a cord over the tops to secure the lids of the cans and started back toward the house.

Just before Zambelli got back inside, I kicked a garbage can twenty feet into air. It showered garbage before it hit the lawn with a loud crash.

"What the hell?" he said. "Must be a bear." He drew a pistol and started walking toward the shed. "Get outa here, you dumb animal!" he shouted.

Who are you calling a dumb animal?

He stopped in the middle of the lawn. "What a damn mess. I'm coming out with a shot gun, dumb-ass bear, you'd better move along."

"Whooup! Whooup!"

"What the hell is that?"

I flung the lid of a garbage can at him. It struck him in the chest and knocked him on his ass. "Damn it!" he coughed, the wind knocked out of him. Zambelli collected himself and picked up the lid, holding it in front of himself as though it were a shield. He moved toward the shed, gun drawn.

But I was no longer there. I took the other garbage can and moved silently, deeper into the woods.

"Where's the other can?" Zambelli asked the darkness. "What kind of bear is this?" He walked into the woods, scanning left to right, just the way cops do in the TV shows I saw from the window outside Christopher's room. That isn't going to get the job done when your attacker is above you, hidden in a tree.

Once he moved beneath the tree, I dumped the contents from the garbage can on him. Zambelli was pelted with chunks of food, cans, bottles, and left-over penne-al la vodka which, by the way, didn't taste half-bad.

"Ahhh!" He cried out and then shot his gun into the woods in confusion. I dropped the can and it landed on his head with a loud crash. He dropped to the floor. *"Owwee!* What the hell!"

Zambelli was terrified and disoriented. He rose to his feet, wiped sauce out of his eyes, turned, and ran toward his house. He slammed into my chest and fell backwards, still holding his gun. "Help! Help me!" He looked up in astonishment and tried to scramble away. I pinned his right arm to the ground with my left foot. I could hear the bones in his arm snapping.

"Oh God! *Ahhh!* You broke my arm! *Ahhh!*"

I lifted him by his shirt collar. The gun fell to the ground; his arm was useless. "Tell me, Zambelli, how does it feel to be disabled?"

"Oh my God!" he wailed. "*Ahhh!*"

"How does it feel to be the one without power? Really need your mob now, don't you?"

His bladder released. "*Ahhh!*"

"But they're not here, Vincent."

"What the hell are you?"

"I am Sasquatch, avenger of the weak."

"What?"

"I've come to adjust your attitude. Open your mind so that you might see the benefits of helping your fellow man."

"You broke my arm! You're an animal!"

"*You're* the animal."

"What're you talking about?"

"You've preyed on people's fears, used their resentments about paying for the needs of others to fuel your desires for power."

"I don't understand. This can't be real."

"I am as real as it gets. You've made war on the weak. Now I've declared war on you."

"You're going to kill me?"

"Were it the bad old days, I'd bash your brains in and rip your guts out. You'd soon be food for worms."

"*Ahhh!*"

"However, I'm much more enlightened now."

"Oh my God, I'm gonna die."

"No, you're just going to learn a little humility."

I placed the palm of my hand on his forehead.

A short while later, Sheriff Jack LaHood walked out of Tina's Coffee Shop, sipping from a paper cup. "What the...Well, what've we here?" He lifted his radio and shouted into it, "Attention all units, deploy to the parking lot of Tina's Coffee Shop with all do haste. I require immediate assistance!"

Another body had been dumped on the roof of his cruiser.

LaHood took out his flash light and walked around the vehicle. He stood on his toes to examine the body on the roof. "This one's still breathing." He spoke into his radio, "We're going to need an ambulance."

"Copy that, Sheriff," a voice answered back. "What's your situation, sir?"

"Got 'nother body layin' on the roof of my car. At least this one's not dead. Smells of garbage, though."

I could hear the wailing sirens of the other cars, which would soon be at the scene.

"Can you identify the body, sir?"

LaHood leaned in with his flash light and burst into laughter. "Yes, I can!"

"Who is it, sir?"

"Mr. Vincent Zambelli."

"What?!"

"You heard that right. He's just coming to...well hello, Vincent. Looks like you had one hell of a campaign party."

Zambelli moaned. "Oh God. My arm's broken."

"Well we're gonna get you some medical attention, no worries. Now, can you explain why you're on the roof of my car?"

"What? What am I doing here?"

"And Vincent, how come you don't have any clothes on?"

Chapter Twenty-Eight

FROM THE DARKNESS of the woods, I watch as Two-Moons is helped onto the back of a flat-bed truck by Useless as Whale Shit. A large group of people has gathered around the Shaman. They wear winter coats to protect themselves against the cold. Some seem to be Native people but others are clearly people from the East. Among them are men with graying beards, donning what look like old military clothing.

"I am Two-Moons of the Red Cedar Tribe. I want to thank you, my brothers and sisters, for joining with us to oppose this infringement on our lands." The crowd clapped, and I continued to watch as Two-Moons spoke, "I will lead you forward toward the construction site and I will lead you in the prayer which we have distributed to you."

A woman joined Two-Moons on the back of the truck. "Friends!" she called out. "As you can see, our opponents have gathered at the barricade that separates us from our own land. The State Police say they and the people who have assembled at the barricade are there to protect the construction site. The police and the observers from the federal government are protecting the wrong side." The crowd broke into cheers. "This land belongs to the tribe, not the pipeline company." People began pumping their fists into the air and shouting in agreement.

Two-Moons tapped his oak stick. "Good people. As you can see, they have brought a water cannon on that army truck. We must expect that they will use it against us. If you are with child or have health concerns, you must stay here. We will feel the power of your words and your support as we move forward."

I looked at the cannon. Grim-looking men in uniform were perched on the truck; they pointed the machine in the direction of the protestors. If that machine shoots water the way guns shoot bullets, this was going to end badly.

Two-Moons, are you mad? You're too old for this. What of *your* health?

"Remember," Two-Moons shouted, "no matter what happens, we must not respond with violence. Let the prayer we say give courage and strength."

Two-Moons was helped down from the truck and the crowd fell in behind him, Whale Shit, and the woman. Slowly they began moving toward the construction area.

A man with a voice machine shouted at them. "People, do not attempt to enter the construction area. To do so is criminal trespass!"

"We are walking on our own lands," Two-Moons shouted back, "the lands of our ancestors.

"You'll be arrested!" the man with the voice machine answered.

"As I walk," Two-Moons shouted.

"As I walk," the people said together.

"The universe walks with me," Two-Moons said.

"The universe walks with me," the people echoed.

"In beauty it walks before me," Two-Moons said.

"In beauty it walks before me," the people responded.

"Do not cross the property boundary!" The man shouted through his voice amplifier.

Two-Moons kept walking toward the barricade. "In beauty it walks behind me."

"In beauty it walks behind me," the people answered.

"Gentlemen," the man shouted to his men, "turn on the pumps!"

"In beauty it walks below me," Two Moons shouted.

"In beauty it walks below me," the crowd said.

"Gentlemen, target the front line of protestors!"

"In beauty it walks above me," Two-Moons said.

"In beauty it walks above me," the people answered.

Whale-Shit trembled but kept walking forward with his uncle.

"Beauty is on every side," the Shaman said.

"Ready, aim..."

"Beauty is on every side," said the people.

"Fire the cannon!"

"As I walk, I walk with beauty," Two-Moons chanted just before the blast from the water cannons blew him and all those around him off their feet.

Bursts of water pounded the Shaman and his people until none could stand. Two-Moons and his followers were forced back from the barricade.

Later that day, I sat on a rock and stared at my reflection in the waters of the Lake of Souls.

Humanity is steeped in darkness. The cruelty of men toward those with less power is unrelenting. There was no justification for what happened at the construction site.

The men with the oil company had even made water, life-giving water, a weapon used to oppress innocent people.

I wanted to rush the men with the water cannons, crush their skulls, and turn the cannon on their leaders.

I wanted to destroy their weapon of desecration and kill them all.

But Two-Moons said that there was to be no violence. Violence does not cure violence.

I thought of Shattuck the Gray and what he would have done. I thought of what he had done all those years ago when he and my ancestors slaughtered those who massacred the Native people. I looked at my reflection in the still water and noticed that I was beginning to show gray on my beard.

I felt my melancholy returning. There are times when I fear that I will simply become a shadow of a shadow, as though I never was. Darkness only leads to more darkness. I wandered through the woods to Christopher's cabin, to seek the light.

Just as I expected, Christopher was out just before sunrise—in his pajamas.

"I thought we agreed that you would stay inside as it gets colder. It's too early for you to be out, little one," I mind-spoke to my young friend.

"I wanted to thank you for helping me. You were so willing to sacrifice yourself."

"I wasn't as willing as you think. A drunken man with a gun is never to be taken lightly."

"Mr. Hasselbeck stayed and talked to mommy for hours. He says that we're lucky to have your presence in our lives. He says that you are different from the others of your kind."

"I fear that he is right."

Christopher picked up a twig and began breaking it into smaller parts. "I know that you're worried."

"Christopher, people are beginning to realize my presence. There are reasons why my kind have lived in the shadows of your world for so long."

"Mommy and I have had to live in the shadows. But some people are beginning to care about us."

"Your mother's courage is stronger than other people's fears. When they see her resolve, they realize your humanity." I looked down. "I am concerned that some men will eventually trap me."

"I don't think that Mr. Hasselbeck wants to trap you. He wants to understand you. If I could talk to him, I would tell him that he must simply walk into your world with an open heart and then he will see you. When we see with our hearts, everything is revealed. That is how you came to me."

I scratched my chin. "You are so wise, little one. Many try to see me through the scope of a rifle. I think that Hasselbeck is, well, interested in your mother…. He said that he didn't want to trap me?"

"He said that to mommy after you left that night. They spent a lot of time talking. Where did you go after the firemen took Clint?"

"I had other business to tend to. That was an interesting night."

"I think Dr. Hasselbeck believes that he is searching for you, but he is really searching for many things in his life."

"Like what?"

"Love and meaning. Many people are looking for those things, but they don't know how to look for them."

"I cannot help Hasselbeck with that."

"Only he can. He needs to look within himself. Then he will see everything more clearly. When you understand yourself, the Creator is revealed."

I handed him another twig to snap. "I have also grappled with these questions. Truth eludes me. I stumble for answers."

"It's the search for truth that matters most. You have worries. I can feel them."

"I fear that a great sacrifice is coming. The Thunderbird is stirring. I don't know what to think and I have people to protect."

"And you fear losing them?"

"Yes, because of my past actions and because of the sins of my ancestors."

"You are not bound by the past. Every person is a new creation. Every day is a new day."

"It's difficult to get the echoes of the past out of your life." I held his hand. "I do not fear death but I fear that if I am discovered, men will come for the rest of my kind. Once they know of us, they will never stop. I have seen what they have done to others who are not quite human."

"What do they do?"

I sighed. "They place them behind bars. Once captured, these beings spend their lives in bondage; they forget what it is to be free."

"I see."

"Men will say that this is not what they intended, but it will still happen. My kind, if they survive, will spend their lives in captivity."

"Your involvement with me has placed this threat before you. If you weren't here protecting me, Hasselbeck would never be able to find you." Christopher gazed into my eyes. "Then you have to let go of me."

"I cannot."

"I would rather live in silence than subject others to such suffering."

"But you've suffered alone for so long. You would spend the rest of your days in silence for my kind?"

Christopher looked calmly into my eyes and nodded. "Yes."

"I cannot accept this fate for you."

"We must stand for what is right, even if we stand alone."

"Christopher, there must be another way." We stood for a moment, looking at each other.

"Sometimes a sacrifice must be made. When we place

the needs of others before ourselves we move closer to the Creator."

"You should not be asked to make this sacrifice."

The sun emerged over the crest of a hill. "Your mother will awaken soon." I carried Christopher back to the cabin and opened the window. "I am not ready to say goodbye to you. I need time to consider your words." I lifted him through the opening.

"We still have time," he said. "Maybe the Creator will reveal a path. A new world is coming. Walk your path in peace, Sasquatch. We shall always share the sky."

I nodded and closed the window.

I was taking too many chances. It wasn't that LaHood had found my foot prints. People had been finding our tracks for years and most people soon forgot about the plaster casts that were made of them.

What if LaHood misunderstood my actions and believed that I was a threat to Christopher? I know what humans, and my kind, are capable of when they have children to protect.

But I was the only one Christopher could fully communicate with. Without me, he would live in the bondage of silence.

For thousands of years, we avoided the humans and retreated into the stillness of the wilderness. Our silence wasn't aloneness. But for Christopher, silence was silence. And yet he would rather endure total isolation than risk my kind by continuing to communicate with me.

He would do this for beings he did not even know.

I had to relay to Two-Moons all of Christopher's words so that he could write them down, as he promised he would. Maybe if people read Christopher's words, they would understand that they had to take care of him. Maybe they would see his humanity. Maybe they would realize their own. Two-Moons seemed to believe it was possible. He held that hope, even though his people had suffered so much at the hands of others who failed to see the humanity in those they saw as different.

I retreated back into the woods and watched the Creator awaken the forest to a new day. "What choices do I have? What is it that you want me to do?"

The Creator was as silent as the forest.

Chapter Twenty-Nine

I RETURNED TO THE construction site and saw two uniformed guards roasting meat over a fire pit. They seemed bored. One sat on a small wooden bench, eating. "This hamburger's great, Billy."

"It's organic."

"Gotta eat healthy," he said, grinning and rubbing his belly. "Stay in shape so we can enjoy them blasting some more gooks if they show up again."

"Blasting old Tonto was just too funny," Billy said. "As I walk, I walk in beauty...then *bam*!" Both men sat laughing.

I wanted to rip their tongues out.

"That tall, scary guy from the federal agency said that he would use the video for training purposes."

The man called Billy got up and urinated on the side of the truck. "I'm gonna go get some more beer. Which agency did he say he was from?"

"I don't recall him saying." He put his hamburger in his plate. "Who is that guy, anyway? He gives me the creeps."

"I dunno. Why don't ya' go up to the company trailer and ask him. Back in a half hour."

I waited until Billy drove away before moving behind the one who remained. I loomed over him while he sat in his chair, stuffing his face.

I kicked the chair out from under him. He landed on his rump in the mud. "What the hell?"

I picked him up by his throat. "You find the abuse of people standing up for their rights and their land amusing?" The man gagged and his eyes bulged. "Let me show you what I think of your machine." I placed my hand on his forehead and erased his memory of me from his weak little mind. Then I pushed him, face first, into the mud.

I climbed onto the back of the truck. "Here's what I, Sasquatch, say to your water weapon." I ripped the machine from its attachments and raised it over my head. I flung it into some metal cans on the other side of the construction site. It landed with such force that the oil drums ruptured and burst into flames. The fire quickly spread, and other cans began exploding.

I ran into the woods and looked back at the conflagration. *"YEEWAAAAH!"* I screamed in triumph.

And that's when I felt his presence for the first time. He was somewhere behind the wall of flames. The man who stood behind the fire had an energy that I had never encountered before. I couldn't see him, but I could feel him.

He was not saddened or angered to see the destruction unfolding in front of him. In fact, he seemed to feed off of it. He delighted in the panic of the workers now running around the construction site trying to control the blaze. As I walked away, I knew that *he* knew the explosion was not caused by a protester.

As the flames rose into the night sky, I could feel his energy calling out to me. I could feel his twisted delight at the destruction unfolding around him, he was feeding off the fears of the men trying to avoid the flames.

He was laughing.

I walked through the woods, worried. Had my actions released a malevolent spirit? Had I unleashed a demon upon my lands?

I went to check on Christopher.

"Stay away, Sasquatch. Joey Hasselbeck and his researchers are camped out with some equipment just off the trail behind my room," Christopher messaged.

"Since when is Hasselbeck *Joey*?"

"That's what mommy calls him."

I wanted to puke when I heard that. I know that they are there, little one. I heard them setting up before night fell."

"You always know when they're in the woods, don't you?"

"I hear all. It's my job to be aware. Humans are rarely aware of how much noise they make. Actually, they're rarely aware of most things."

"It's kind of funny, because they go to such lengths to be secretive."

"It's funny when men hunt with cameras. It's a different matter when they hunt with guns."

Mongo and Hasselbeck were sitting on chairs behind some cloth that they believed concealed them. From time to time, their heads popped up and they peered into the darkness through night vision goggles.

"Dude, should we do some tree knocks?" Mongo asked Hasselbeck.

"I don't think so. This one seems to come by the cabin if and when he chooses."

"We close to its water supply? A good food source?"

"I scoped out the area for three hours today. There's not a lot here to attract a Big Foot, really. I did find some ancient Native rock art."

"That's kinda cool," Mongo grunted.

"Marianna said that there was no record of the carving and that the archeological society would be out here tomorrow to look at it."

"Outstanding. You discovered an archeological site."

"Yeah, but we're Big Foot hunters. We're supposed to find a Squatch."

"Maybe he appreciates the art," Mongo laughed.

"Maybe it's the smell of food from the cabin. The place was empty for a long time before Marianna and Christopher moved in. Maybe the return of human activity drew him in," Hasselback mused more seriously.

"A Squatch who follows his belly," Mongo continued to joke. He exhaled some steam out of his mouth. "I'm freezing. You smell snow coming?"

Hasselbeck peered into the darkness. "I don't really get what's drawing him to this area."

Marianna walked quietly down the path holding two cups.

"Hey guys. I brought some hot coffee."

"You're a life saver," Hasselbeck said, smiling.

"Thanks, Ranger Carino," Mongo said before sipping from the cup.

"See anything?" she asked.

"It's been quiet," Hasselbeck answered, looking around. "It's still beautiful here."

"I know that the cabin is run down," Marianna said. "But this is the best place I've ever had for myself and Christopher."

"I like your kid," Mongo said. "You look into his eyes and you can see he's got stuff going on."

"His teachers say that, too. I just wish that he could talk."

I wish that too, Marianna.

"I think he will someday," Hasselbeck said. "He's got stuff to say. I can feel that. There's a sparkle to him."

"There's a new kind of therapy that a specialist in Seattle will show me how to use with Christopher. From what I've seen on-line, it might help him get language going."

Hasselbeck rubbed his beard. "What do you need to do to get him there?"

"I need to work more over-time. I was doin' okay with that until my principle baby-sitter went psycho."

"We'll watch Christopher," Hasselbeck volunteered.

"I'm in," Mongo added. "I bet Rachel will help out, too, once she's on her feet more."

"You would do that for us?"

Both men nodded.

"You fed us," Mongo said smiling. "Feed a Squatch hunter, and you can't get rid of us."

Marianna's eyes misted. "I don't know what to say."

Hasselbeck smiled. "Just say yes."

They hugged. I felt as though my brains would explode in a fit of rage.

"Christopher's really worth it. A few months ago, though, he was driving me and everyone crazy."

I heard a car driving up the road to the cabin.

"Why's that?" Hasselbeck asked.

"He was leaving school and the cabin and he was wandering. The school couldn't always keep track of him, and I was on the verge of getting in trouble with LaHood. Christopher was having seizures, too. It was awful."

I heard the car park and someone get out of the vehicle. Someone else was joining the group.

Mongo peered over the cloth with his night vision goggles. "Nuthin'."

Hasselbeck sipped some coffee and continued with Marianna. "But things got better?"

"Yeah. Right after the time LaHood deployed the entire Sheriff's Department to find Christopher one stormy night after he wandered away from the cabin. The woods were filled with people looking for Christopher. I can't tell you how terrified I was. No one knows that dread, that fear of having your child wander away."

"That's awful. Thank God the deputies found him."

"Actually, they found Christopher asleep in the back seat of LaHood's car. He was right under their noses all the time."

"Really? What was he doing in LaHood's car?"

"Sleeping. He hasn't had a seizure since that day."

Mongo got out of his chair and looked at Marianna closely. "You sayin' that Christopher ended up in the Sheriff's car while everyone was out looking for him?"

Hasselbeck grabbed Mongo's shoulder. "Mongo, do you think that..."

"...a Squatch put Christopher in my car?" LaHood finished the thought. "I'm bettin' that it's the same one that dumped Vincent Zambelli on the roof of my car night 'fore last."

Everyone turned to LaHood.

"What?!" Hasselbeck exclaimed.

"It sounds like I've happened into this conversation at the right moment. Been a lot of odd events around Deception Falls for months now."

"I'd say so," Hasselbeck agreed.

LaHood looked at Marianna. "And I think that it's all tied to a Big Foot who's protecting you and your son."

Marianna's eyes grew large. "Sheriff, why would a Big Foot do that?"

"I don't know. But that's what I'm thinkin' been happenin' here. That's why we found Romeo up in the tree back there. And I think Vincent Zambelli pissed the Squatch off too, because he ended up naked and unconscious on the roof of my car. He couldn't remember nuthin'."

Marianna frowned. "Zambelli was *naked*?"

"Not 'zactly an image I want in my mind either, Marianna. Dr. Hasselbeck, I'm thinkin' that this Squatch has been sendin' me some personal communications. Not sure he likes me too much, though. Anyway, Zambelli's in the hospital and out of the mayoral race."

"Wow!" Mongo gasped, trying to grasp the whole of what LaHood was saying.

"Protecting me too?"

"Marianna," LaHood took off his hat. "Think 'bout what happened to that thug rapist in the Saddle Brook Parking Lot."

Marianna covered her mouth. "Oh my God!"

Hasselbeck drank more coffee. "What are you talking about? What happened in the parking lot?"

"Dr. Hasselbeck, this park ranger is one of the toughest women I ever met," he nodded at Marianna. "You don't meet this kinda person every day. She saved a young woman from a vicious rapist few months back."

"I was doing my job," Marianna said.

"Your back-up was miles away. That son-of-a-bitch was big, crank-crazed, and armed. I wouldn't blame any officer for backin' off 'til help arrived. You stood your ground. Alone."

"That young girl was terrified," Marianna added quietly.

Hasselbeck couldn't take his eyes off Marianna. "With everything you deal with...wow."

"Joey," Marianna whispered. "The man's head exploded. The autopsy showed that a rock hit his skull at over a hundred miles an hour. He was killed instantly."

"Holy shit," Mongo gasped.

Marianna dropped into Hasselbeck's chair. "I get it now. The Big Foot was protecting me. And he protects Christopher."

Enough.

I ran to Hasselbeck's base camp with purple rage burning in my guts. Hasselbeck and his crew had done more than ruin the peace of my domain. Now they were interfering with my relationships.

These nitwits couldn't protect Christopher. They couldn't even protect themselves. It was time to get them out of the Big Foot hunting business.

I turned Hasselbeck's car over and ripped all the pipes out of its underbelly. I broke the windows of Mongo's research van. I stuffed tree branches into the van and tore the steering wheel out. I split the seats open and tore out all the stuffing.

I ripped their tents to shreds and tore up their sleeping bags. I threw their provisions all over the camp site.

I threw the extra night vision goggles into a pond. Then I took out the stupid circular listening devices and shattered then on rocks.

Stay away from my people, Hasselbeck. You've been warned.

Chapter Thirty

THE NEXT MORNING, I woke to a snow storm and to Hasselbeck walking down a trail toward my sleeping nest by the Lake of Souls. He was shrieking.

"Come out, you hairy bastard!"

Oh, you've got to be kidding. Hasselbeck was calling me out. 'Joey' Hasselbeck was walking into *my* domain and challenging *me* – on sacred ground!

"You don't have the balls to come out and confront me, you coward!"

I shoved a mid-sized tree over to warn this chucklehead that he was pushing his luck. The tree landed with a thunderous crash.

Hasselbeck froze in place. "I know you're strong, but you destroyed my camp site when we were at the cabin because you don't have the balls to confront me, you beast!"

I cleared some snow and collected the rocks underneath. If this fool didn't learn from what happened to that deviant maniac in the parking lot, then he deserved to die. Small rocks first. I would pelt him with dozens of small rocks. Hasselbeck would die a slow death by a hundred pelts.

"You wrecked my life's work you lumbering creep!"

Your life's work wasn't worth a hill of shit. How dare you challenge me! You will linger and suffer before I kill you. I want you to know that you're doomed. Awaiting death is worse than death itself. You've screwed with the wrong Big Foot.

Hasselbeck pounded a pine tree with a stick, showering himself with snow. "I'm gonna kick your ass you son-of-a-bitch!"

"Whooup!"

A rock hit him in the back. "Ahh!" Another smacked him in the leg. "Damn!" He took out a small phone and punched some numbers. "I'm not backing down!" he screamed into the cold air.

Yeah, what are you going to do? Call for help on your puny phone? It's just me and you now, Joey. No one is coming to your aid out here. I'm going to crush your testicles. You'll beg for mercy. And then I'll kill you - slowly. You're going to die a horrible death, Hasselbeck.

"Whooup!"

A rock hit him in the chest, knocking him on his rump. "Ahhh! I'm not afraid of you. Come out and face me, you smelly ape!"

Enough.

"WHAAHOO!"

I burst upon him in an avalanche of snow. Hasselbeck's eyes bulged as I lifted him off the ground—by his throat.

"It's you who smells. You've never fooled me, not for a minute, Hasselbeck."

"Gack...gack," he choked.

"How dare you come here and challenge me. You'll suffer an excruciating death for this affront!"

"Let me...*gack*...let me talk!"

"I don't care what you say. You're a dead man."

"You can speak!"

"Always the stunned amazement over intelligence and language. You think words mean intelligence? Words, words, words. Do you know why your kind evolved speech?"

"No." *Gack, gack.*

"So you could lie to each other! Yes, I can speak." I pulled him closer. "And know this—my voice will be the last you hear. You should've listened to what LaHood and Marianna told you about the killing in that parking lot. Happy now that you've finally found Big Foot?"

"Why'd you destroy my camp?"

"Because I chose too. You screwed with my people!"

"You're wrong! I want to help them..." *Gack.*

"You people always say that before you wreck the lives of others. Scientists are just the latest in a long line of criminals who slaughter the innocent in the name of progress. 'Oh, but we wanted to help. We wanted progress. Our intentions were good.' Then the bodies begin to pile up. I'm going to rip your guts out and feed them to other predators."

"I was going to sell my equipment so Marianna could take Christopher to a therapist who could help him talk."

I let go and he crumpled into the snow, coughing and hacking.

"Kill me if you want. But I love Marianna and want to help her care for her son."

"What do you know of love?" I screamed so loudly that snow tumbled off tree branches.

"I know it because I feel it. Why are you protecting them?"

I lifted him off the ground by his hair and glared into his eyes. "If you sold your equipment, you couldn't hunt me anymore. You'd never do that."

"I swear to God, that was my plan. This hurts like hell, please put me down." I dropped him. "I'm willing to sacrifice everything for them. Know that before you kill me."

I loomed over him. "If I don't kill you, you'll tell everyone about me. My domain will be flooded with Big Foot hunters and my kind will lose their freedom."

"I understand and..."

I put my foot into his stomach and pushed him into the snow-covered ground, hard. "No, you don't! People like you have never understood, never known what it is to be hunted, to be feared and loathed, to be different and to live in the shadows, to live as Christopher has had to live."

Hasselbeck's face turned red and he was about to lose consciousness. "He can communicate with you. My God, that's it."

I took the pressure off him and stepped away. "I am the only one who can hear his words." The wind blew snow into my eyes as I looked up into the stormy sky. "Sometimes, I wonder if I am cursed, and yet I feel that the Creator wanted me for this purpose."

"How is this possible?"

"I don't know. And I don't know why I was chosen for this." I looked down at Hasselbeck and shrugged. "The Creator speaks through him. And if your people heard his words, his message could change your world. Maybe then you'd stop trying to destroy mine." I sat on a rock and buried my face in my hands. "Men do not know how to listen. We are surrounded by the beauty of the Creator's vision but we don't see it. And I have been no different." I looked Hasselbeck in the eyes. "I am sorry about your equipment."

"At least I finally discovered some things of importance before I died," he said. "Marianna, Christopher, and, finally, you."

"You've discovered nothing. I'm just another kind of primate. But love for these people, well, that's something of worth."

Hasselbeck staggered to his feet. "I do love them. They're worth the risks we both took. They're worth my life. Kill me if you have to, but please don't torture me."

I shook my head and grabbed his arm. "You will die someday, Joseph Hasselbeck." I placed my hand on his forehead. "But not on this day."

Later that night I walked into Two-Moon's cabin and woke him up.

"Old one, I need you to write."

"You startled me, brother. Is something wrong?"

"Yes. The end is coming. There will soon be a great sacrifice."

Two-Moons rose and wiped the sleep from his eyes. "How can I help?"

"Write my words. No – they are not my words. They are the words of Christopher of Cascadia, who is loved by God."

The Shaman took a pad from the top of his refrigerator and lit the lantern that was on his table. "I am old, my brother. I write slowly."

"Do your best. These are the words that we were both meant to write down. This is why you came into my father's domain all those years ago. I see that now."

"I was so young, but I remember it as if it were yesterday."

"Why is it that you are called *Two-Moons*? Most of your people have names like the ones used by the people from the east. Is it a mystical name?"

"My mother was in labor with me for two long nights. Nothing mystical, but the name suits the Shaman role, don't you think?"

I laughed. "So much of life is defined by the labels we use, isn't it?'

"But more by what we do, my brother. I remember your father. He drew me to the forest and to The Great Spirit through dreams. I needed that. My people needed that. They still do."

"Without our dreams, we are nothing."

"I was ready to sacrifice myself to bring our people together again."

"It seems that is also to be my job. Write this: The Creator is all around us, but people do not see him. To see the Creator, you must first..."

"Speak more slowly, my brother, I am old."

"...you must first come to know yourself."

Two-Moons wrote as quickly as he could.

"To overcome anger, you must help people in need, even when doing so is at great cost." I watched him write. "It's important to understand your own faults so that you can understand others."

Two-Moons nodded peacefully. "Yes, this is good."

"Blessed are they who are kind, even when no one else sees them being kind." He looked at me and nod-ded.

"Blessed are the hunted, for they shall taste true freedom."

He moved the pad closer to his face. "Go on."

"Everything that is created is new and unique and loved by those who created it. We look very different, but we are all connected through time and blood."

Tears rolled down his old face but his eyes sparkled with joy.

"We are all ancient. But each one of us is new. The earth is ancient, but every day is a new creation. Every person is a new creation, but people do not always see this."

"This child is a spirit."

"Violence cannot be cured with violence.... Blessed are those who overcome their shadow, they shall be filled with light."

"He is right."

"Blessed are those who protect the weak, they shall be given the sky. The sky shelters us all. We are all broth-ers and sisters and we all share the sky."

Two-Moons smiled. "We are lucky to have had the lives we've had, my brother."

I nodded. "Write this: We must stand for what is right, even if we stand alone." I cleared my throat. "Let me tell you how the world was created. In the beginning, there was only darkness. The creator wanted to fill the void, so he made the earth, the sky, the stars and the waters...."

Chapter Thirty-One

I GAZED DOWN upon a snow-covered valley as the sun rose in the freezing sky. The woods were full of people searching for Joseph Hasselbeck. I counted fourteen people slogging through the snow; steam from their breath hung in the still morning air.

Marianna and Mongo were following Hasselbeck's tracks toward the Lake of Souls. LaHood and his men were fanning out behind them.

"Joe!" Mongo shouted. His voice echoed down the canyon.

"Joey!" Marianna yelled. "Mongo, his tracks run up the path that goes to Round Lake. But the wind caused some drifting and snow is covering some of the footprints."

"Tough conditions, but at least the snow isn't too deep."

Marianna was almost out of breath. "We don't get that much snow 'cause we're near the coast. But this winter's been a cold one; temperatures dropped into the teens last night, Mongo. He's really at risk of exposure."

Mongo put his hand on her shoulder. "Marianna, we'll find him."

"I just don't know what he was thinking about. I wish that he was thinking about me. If he had been, he wouldn't have done this."

"Well, actually, I think he was thinking about you, Marianna, sort of. Joe!"

"Joey!" she shouted.

"JOE!" Mongo shouted again. "I told him to calm down, but he was so pissed off about the damaged equipment."

"That's no excuse. Men just can't lay it on the old, *'I got pissed off and went bat-shit'* routine. I've had enough of that."

"Actually, what he planned to do was..."

"The tracks are gone. We lost him." Marianna was on the verge of tears. "We have to find him. Mongo, I think I love him."

"Let's keep looking up this trail."

"I could kill him right now. I finally find a good man and he pulls this."

"He knows how to survive in the woods."

"What if this *thing* killed him? You should've seen what happened to that criminal's head. A quarter of his skull was blown off."

Hasselbeck appeared before them at the top of trail. "I'm here."

Mongo dialed his phone while Marianna ran up the trail to Hasselbeck. "Sheriff, we found him. He looks okay..."

The couple embraced, and Marianna kissed Hasselbeck's tired, bruised face, over and over. "Thank God. Thank God."

"I'm okay. I missed you, too," Hasselbeck smiled. "Thanks for looking for me."

"Dude," Mongo shouted. "You alright?"

Marianna continued kissing him.

"Yeah. Cold, but functional."

Mongo sighed. "What the hell were you thinking about?"

"I was pissed, so I went out to confront the beast for trashing our equipment."

"It's just stuff!" Marianna shouted. "You took on this giant Big Foot because he trashed your toys?"

"Well, actually, I wanted to..."

"How many more men do I have meet who act like idiots?"

"Mongo and I were going to sell some of the *stuff* and give you the money so you could take Christopher to Seattle to see that therapist."

Marianna turned to Mongo. "Why didn't you tell me about that?"

"Yes, Sheriff, he's ambulatory," Mongo said into his phone. "Hey, he's your boyfriend. Telling you was supposed to be his job."

"You'd do that for me? For us?"

"Yes. I love you."

Mongo turned bright red and shouted into his phone, "Sheriff, could you please come get me out of here?"

A short time later, Hasselbeck sat in the back seat of LaHood's car, drinking hot coffee. LaHood was angry. "That was a shit-all stupid maneuver, Hasselbeck."

"I realize that now."

"This animal's no joke."

"Oh, I know."

"If I could, I'd charge him in two homicides. Although Judge Holland's so liberal that she'd likely allow the beast to make bail."

Hasselbeck's eyes widened. "Two?"

"There was another incident the night of the parking lot killing. A drug dealer must have picked a fight with Big Foot 'cause he got killed, too."

"Damn!" Mongo said.

Marianna glared at LaHood. "I heard that was a shooting."

"It was. But before my deputy shot the guy, it seems the dealer was involved in some sort of confrontation with an unknown being who was hurling rocks. The drug dealer had a rock embedded in his guts." He turned to Hasselbeck. "No more Squatch huntin'."

"Awesome!" Mongo leaned into LaHood. "Squatches use stones as tools, as weapons. "I've seen kills in which animals have their skulls crushed from impacts. Squatches have become really good at using rocks."

Hasselbeck opened his shirt. "Look. I've got a welt on my chest. I've got other ones as well."

"Oh my God," Marianna said.

Hasselbeck downed more coffee. "They use sticks as clubs, too, Sheriff. They're amazingly resourceful. Perfectly adapted to their environment – and to evading us."

LaHood looked at Hasselbeck's chest. "And killin'. You made contact with it?"

"I think I did."

"What do ya mean by that?"

"I think I did because I can't remember anything after I saw the lake."

LaHood looked at Marianna. "Just like what happened to Clint."

"I woke this morning on a fairly comfortable bed of pine branches between some rocks."

Mongo unzipped his jacket. "Dude, you slept in a Squatch nest! I'm so freakin' jealous."

"He covered me with pine and moss, too - remarkably effective against the cold. I really appreciate this coffee!"

Mongo pulled LaHood aside. "Sheriff, I want to go back on the trail and see that nest."

"No more Squatch huntin'!" LaHood seethed. "Someone else is gonna get killed."

"Marianna," Hasselbeck whispered. "I have to tell you something - later."

LaHood turned back to Hasselbeck, scowling. "You're lucky you're in one piece. The town oughta take the cost of this search for you outa your ass."

"I'm sorry, sir."

Marianna smiled at LaHood. "Well at least you don't have another dead body stuck on your car, Jack."

"Guess so," LaHood nodded. "Hey, why aint you dead?"

Hasselbeck took a gulp of coffee. "One reason: he chose not to kill me."

Chapter Thirty-Two

"SASQUATCH," CHRISTOPHER messaged me, "Joey played the tape recording of your conversation with him from his phone. I'm really glad that you didn't kill him. You overcame your anger with him. I'm proud of you."

"What?"

"He said that he realized that he had been recording your meeting after he woke up this morning. Everybody wants to protect you and your people now."

"That lying, deceiving, rat! I'm going to rip his tongue out. It wasn't a meeting, it was a confrontation. He's lucky to be breathing. He had no right to do that!"

"Joey says that…"

"Stop calling him Joey—he's Hasselbeck. Soon to be Hasselbeck, the Dead Big Foot Hunter."

"He said that he thought that he was going to be killed and that he just wanted people to know what happened to him."

I started moving toward the cabin as the sun fell behind Mount Olympus. "Is he still there?"

"Yes. Mongo left to visit Rachel in town and we're finishing dinner."

"It's his last meal."

"He wasn't being deceptive. He's a good person."

"I'm not so sure."

"He is. He wants to help."

"Then he should prove it. All right, I won't kill him, but I need that phone. I intend to take it."

I heard a hawk screeching from above. It was the same hawk that appeared to me the day I saved Christopher.

"Sasquatch, Clint is on the porch. He has a gun!"

"What?"

"Mommy and Joey don't see him."

The hawk circled above.

I heard gun fire coming from the area around the cabin and tore toward it. "I'm coming. Tell your mother to shoot back!"

"I can't talk!"

"I'm on the way. Stay alive. No matter what happens, stay alive!"

"Clint is in the house!"

Another shot. "Get out of there!"

"We're climbing out my window. Mommy's crying. I'm scared."

I reached down and picked up a thick branch. "Run to the Thunderbird rock. I can stop him there."

"Joey called the Sheriff from his phone. We're running away from the cabin."

"Keep running. Does your mother have her gun?"

"Yes."

"Tell her to shoot Clint!"

"I can't!"

"She has to!"

"I can't tell her because I can't talk!"

I was running as fast as I could. I heard the hawk screeching angrily in the darkening gloom.

"Clint sees us!" Another shot rang out. "He's shooting at Joey!"

I could hear shouts from the two men. Then more shots. I moved behind a stand of pine trees as another round rang out. I heard Hasselbeck screaming in agony. I looked around a tree to see Hasselbeck, sitting against a tree, bleeding from his shoulder. Clint stood over him.

"Took my woman, you son-of-a-bitch," Clint raged.

"You lost her, you idiot."

Clint swayed in drunken anger. "The only idiot that I see is bleedin' out into the snow. I'm gonna kill her and her retard son and come back for you."

Hasselbeck lunged and the two men wrestled in the snow. Then Clint smacked Hasselbeck's face with the back end of his gun. A moment later, Hasselbeck lay unconscious. Clint stood up and started following the tracks made by Marianna and Christopher.

I knew where those tracks would lead. Christopher and Marianna would have to confront Clint or jump off the cliff.

I followed noiselessly as Clint followed the trail.

Marianna suddenly fired at him, but missed.

"Your gun's only got six rounds, Darlin'!" he shouted. "You've only got one left."

"Yeah, but I'm not drunk like you. I'll kill you, Clint."

"I've got five rounds and another magazine. And another and another."

"Leave us alone!"

"You know I can't do that, Darlin'. I loved you too much. You dumped me for that crypto-botanist."

"He's a crypto-zoologist, you idiot!"

"I don't care what he was. I'll could kill you for leaving me."

Marianna and Christopher were now at the edge of the cliff. "You don't know what love is. Leave or I'll kill you, I swear to God!"

"Loved you so much. I'm the only one who can have you. If I can't have you, I'll kill you. Then I'll kill myself."

"You need help. You're sick!"

Clint laughed demonically. "I am sick. So, so sick. You're my medicine."

"No, I'm not. I'm done with you!"

Clint screamed, "You took up with that loser while I was in the hospital!" He fired another round.

"Back off, or I'll shoot."

"You've never killed. You won't start now."

Marianna shielded Christopher who was crouched down in the snow. "Get out of here or I'll shoot."

"No, you won't." He emerged into the clearing and stood across from them. "You don't have what it takes to kill. I know you, 'cause I've slept with you. A man knows his woman. Now come help me dump your new boyfriend's body."

Marianna collapsed onto the snow-covered forest floor. "You killed Joey! You bastard."

Clint moved toward her. "Got what was comin' to him."

Marianna gritted her teeth. "Now you're gettin' what's coming to you." She rose, aimed, and fired. Clint spun and fell face down into the snow.

Marianna grabbed Christopher's hand and started running back down the trail.

Clint suddenly reached and grabbed Christopher's leg. Marianna and Christopher tumbled to the ground as Clint rose. Spitting blood and holding his chest, he drew his gun again. "I'm doin' your son," he screamed. "Then I'll kill you!"

"WHAAHOO!"

I swung down from a tree and landed between Marianna and Clint. I struck Clint across the jaw with my club, but it wasn't the devastating blow I wanted. Clint spun around, shooting his gun.

I felt a burning sensation in my throat. Before he regained his balance, I swung again and shattered Clint's skull. The force of my blow sent him spiraling backwards over the edge of the cliff.

Chapter Thirty-Three

I LAY IN THE SNOW, looking at the sunlight fade from the sky. Marianna is kneeling over me, crying and pressing a cloth against my neck. I hear the siren of LaHood's car wailing in the distance. I lean up to talk to Marianna. "Let me die."

But the words won't come out.

Darkness.

Hasselbeck kneels in the snow next to me. He's still bleeding from his shoulder and has an enormous, swollen black eye, yet he's holding the cloth against my wound, too. "We're going to get help."

Hasselbeck has finally proven that he is a real person. I was wrong about him. "Joseph, let me die. Take care of Marianna and Christopher."

But the words won't come out.

"He's trying to say something," Hasselbeck shouts.

LaHood appears. "He's a killer. Get away from him!"

I see LaHood standing over me, pistol drawn. "Listen to LaHood. Let me die."

But the words won't come out.

"Keep the kid away from him!" LaHood shouts.

But Christopher pulls away from Marianna and touches my hand. Once again, I feel his incredible energy. "Thank you, Sasquatch. You saved us."

"It is you who saved me, little one."

"Please don't die."

"This is our way, to die protecting those we care for."

"Without you, no one hears my words."

"The Shaman has every word you spoke to me. Go to the Shaman."

I pointed at Hasselbeck. "Go to the Shaman."

But the words wouldn't come out.

Darkness.

I hear the sound of mourning cries echo through the domain. My people are pounding oak as never before.

LaHood stares at Marianna in astonishment. "Do you think they'll attack?"

"I don't know what to think. I'm going with Joey in the ambulance."

The Thunderbird circles above as night overtakes the woods. He is surrounded by a warm blue light. Then he is gone.

The blue light is from a sky machine.

Darkness.

My body is rising into the sky. Although everything around me is dark, I am being drawn up to a light in the sky. Is this what it is to die?

I try to move my arms but I realize that I am strapped in a metal bed. I am unable to move.

More pounding echoes through the domain.

"We will avenge you, Sasquatch," Shattuck the Gray messages. "Know that the day is coming when we shall kill them all."

Screams and howls from other dominant males shake the very foundation of Mount Olympus as I continue to rise into the blackness.

From above, I see a human wearing a helmet. Is this

one of the actors from the television show that Christopher watches?

"This cage will barely hold him," he shouts. "What if he revives?"

"Then you'll have to shoot him. I can't have this thing going berserk in my chopper."

I am pulled inside the sky machine. I look into the eyes of the human handling the metal bed I'm lying in. I can sense his terror. I feel something stab my arm, then an odd floating sensation.

Darkness.

I awake to a white light shining in my eyes and to a searing pain in my throat. I want to scream but no sound comes out.

What is this place? The light bounces glaringly off the white walls. I am surrounded by people wearing white coats and white masks. I am surrounded by white. I want to get up, but I can't move. I feel as though I'm watching myself, as though I were on Christopher's television.

"He's remarkable," someone says.

Another voice, "I guess all the people I made fun of were right."

"Do you think he'll survive?"

"Lost a lot of blood, but he's got a lot more blood than a human does. I don't know."

"Where's he gonna end up?"

"He's from our area. We should be allowed to keep him here."

"You heard the administrator. Some federal government officials are coming from Olympia to make those decisions. We'll know soon enough."

"He's awake and moving a little. Let's put him out. He's gotta be in agony."

Darkness.

I hear voices around me again. Hasselbeck, LaHood, and Marianna have been close.

"What is the plan for release?" Hasselbeck asks.

"That's not your concern."

"Yes, it is," Marianna says.

"The Governor is evaluating the situation."

"It's not a situation. It's about the right way to treat an intelligent creature," Hasselbeck states firmly.

"It's an animal."

"We're all animals. You, me, we're all animals. This one happens to also be remarkably like us."

"I respect your advocacy and your passion."

"Don't try to placate me. Your zoo claims to take pride in its wildlife recovery and release program."

"He saved our lives!" Marianna shouted. "A regular *animal* wouldn't do that."

"You've never heard of a loyal dog that fights to protect his owners? Are you saying that those dogs are *persons*?"

"He took a bullet for my son. Most humans wouldn't have done that."

"I understand your feelings and..."

"You don't understand anything," Marianna interrupted.

"Look, the Governor is evaluating the situation. The discovery of this species is a huge event. I'm sure that you understand that, Doctor Hasselbeck."

I hear a fist pound a desk. "This isn't right!"

"Please, Doctor Hasselbeck..."

Exhaustion and darkness overtake me.

I awake to see blue sky at the end of a narrow hall. The hall is white and cave-like. But caves aren't white.

I can move my arms enough to pull myself up to a sitting position. Dizziness overtakes me. My hands, are shaking. There are cloths around my neck. I realize that the humans have put them there to cover my wound.

I see a bowl of water which I reach to pick up. I realize, with horror, that my arms are chained. I have to lean to drink from the bowl, and lap the water like a dog. The water burns my throat; I cough and spit up blood from my wounds.

There's a sliding sound that comes from behind me. I turn my head to see human eyes glaring at me through a narrow slit in a large metal door. I glare back.

Slowly, I rise to my feet. I brace myself against the wall and stagger toward the doorway. I just want to see the sky and smell the forest air. If I get outside, I can signal my people to let them know that I am here. But as I get close to the exit, the chains pull tight. I can't get near the doorway.

Then I see it. There's a huge, black, reinforced-metal cage, thirty feet tall, sitting just beyond the exit. The sign hanging from the steel bars reads, *Orangutan Habitat Enclosure*.

Chapter Thirty-Four

IMPRISONED IN MY cell, I hear all. The Cascadia County Zoo administrators continue their meetings about my fate.

"I just don't think we're equipped to deal him," the one named Vito says.

"I know that, but a live Big Foot is the attraction of the century," the one called Evans says. "This one animal will solve our budget problems. We can save this zoo when we become an international site of tourism *and* scientific study."

"I think the Governor's people are right. We should turn him over to the Capital Zoo in Olympia. He broke Orenstein's fingers yesterday."

Orenstein had it coming. The white coated bastard's been injecting me with drugs every day. He's even putting drugs in my food dish. I was woozy when I rolled over on his hand as he was giving me another injection.

"I feel badly about what happened to that old man, but think of the future of our program."

"What about the Shaman? That guy's outside every

day, chanting. He's giving me the creeps. *Free C'iatqo! Free C'iatqo!"*

"I told you to have LaHood arrest the damn guy."

"LaHood won't touch him. He told me to pound sand. He says that animal will eventually kill us all if we don't free him like Hasselbeck says."

"He can screw off."

I sit in chains, a prisoner, starring out of a small window at Tang's artificial tree.

Where is that red-haired, odd-ball, Tang, the Orangutan? I tried messaging him. I can feel his presence; he's somewhere in the building. But he won't answer me.

My wounds are healing but I'm miserable. The food is lousy and many days I refuse to eat it. It sits in the tray on the sandy floor until they take it away. I'm losing weight.

And I still can't talk or call to my people. They don't know that I'm still alive. Unless I can get out into the open air, they won't be able to connect to my thoughts.

They don't know that I'm here.

I know understand, now, what life has been like for Christopher. Now I understand what silence is really like. It casts a pall over your existence and lets people render you invisible.

At night I hear his voice in my dreams. His words bring me comfort. His words are all that I have. "I look to God to stir compassion in my brothers and sisters to see our shared humanity...."

Down the hall, I hear the administrators talking.

"That weirdo, Hasselbeck, has served us with papers demanding the Big Foot's freedom," Vito says. "The Red Cedar tribe is signing the petition. Protests are planned. Bastard's playing hard ball."

"The Governor is calling some lawyers and some bigwigs from D.C. to resolve all of the disputes," Evans responds. "Some brilliant, charismatic conflict resolution guy is supposed to come in tomorrow and broker a deal."

"He'd better be a genius. Hasselbeck is threatening to go to the press."

The next morning, Orenstein visits me with a young male aide. The old white-coated creep and his young assistant are shaking as they enter. I glare at them. They stay close to the exit, beyond my reach. The chains restrict me to the middle of the room. The aide puts down a food tray, then pushes it closer to me with a broom stick.

I lunge forward and both men flee the room. "The food is crap!" I try to yell.

But the words won't come out. I throw the food dish at the door.

The aide looks in on me a short while later. "Don't like the food?"

No shit. Boy, you're a smart one. Move a little closer, punk, so I can relieve you of your liver and munch on that. That will freak out Evans and Vito. The zoo administrators will have to put me down. And then I'll be free.

"What do you want to eat?" he asks, remaining just outside my reach.

I motion with my hands for him to move a little closer.

"No way, big guy. I saw what you did to Doctor Orenstein."

That was a misunderstanding. I know that I broke two of his fingers. However, if it were the bad old days, I would've snapped his neck. I've not been on my game lately.

He smiles nervously. "What can I get you to eat?"

Well, your liver, but since that's not an option, some salmon would be sublime. But how do I explain that to him?

I bend over and draw the outline of a salmon in the sand. Then I point to it as if to say, "Got it, shit-head?"

"Oh my God!" he bolts from the room and locks the door.

Within a few minutes, Orenstein is back with a dart

gun. He's going to drug me, again. They inject me with needles from gun-like devices. Is there nothing on earth that men won't twist into a weapon? I pound the walls with my fists. Plaster chunks break from the walls and dust sprinkles down on me from the ceiling.

Orenstein fires the gun and a dart punctures my thigh. "The ketamine will calm him down," he says. I fall to the floor and lose consciousness as I see Orenstein's foot wipe away the outline of the fish in the sand.

I wake later that night and can almost see the light of the moon through my window. The drug has left me listless. My mouth is dry, and though my thirst consumes me, there is no water in my dish.

Orenstein is drugging me to control my behavior, to keep the others from seeing my intelligence, to keep them from seeing my humanity.

Men and their drugs. And their guns. And their desire to control everything.

I, Sasquatch, am now something else to be controlled. I want to fight back but Christopher's words haunt me. "Violence does not cure violence."

"Blessed are the hunted, for they shall taste freedom."

When, my friend?

I pray for death, but death eludes me.

Chapter Thirty-Five

I AWAKE SUDDENLY, feeling ill. I sniff the air because there is something in the zoo that I had not sensed before. My eyes dart around my enclosure. It is dark.

Then I realize what it is. I realize *who* it is. It is the man who stood laughing as fire raged around him at the construction site.

That man was now only feet away from me.

And I was in chains.

"I am Adolphus Wolf. I represent the interests of those concerned with the present situation."

"Do you work for the federal government?" Hasselbeck asks.

"You could say that," Wolf responds. "I am here to protect certain interests and resolve disagreements between parties."

"You're not getting my question. Who pays you?"

Hasselbeck has benefitted from my work with him. He's turning into a real man.

I could hear this Wolf fellow chuckle. "Don't worry, Doctor Hasselbeck, I get paid. May I have your name, sir?"

"I am Two-Moons. You must free C'iatqo."

You tell them old one!

"Is he the property of your people?" Wolf asks.

"A Big Foot is not property. He is a free being. What you are you doing is offensive."

Evans cut in. "Our zoo has cared for the Big Foot. It's costing us a fortune, and we're a financially stressed facility. Our primate program has already been cut to the bone."

"Gentlemen," Wolf says, "the Governor believes that the Big Foot, like all other wild life within the state's boundaries, is the property of the state. Since your tribe doesn't claim any rights over this creature then..."

Two-Moons taps his walking stick on the floor. "You're not listening."

"People, this is a complicated, emotional matter," Wolf intercedes. "We all want to do the right thing. A new discovery like this one challenges us to do so."

"I think the public would be outraged by the imprisonment of a thinking creature," Hasselbeck says. "We sought the zoo's assistance in healing the Big Foot. What's gone on since that day is shocking."

"Do you have concerns about the care of this animal at our facility?" Evans asks.

"Yes. Why haven't you allowed us to see him?"

It's Marianna.

"My son and I want to thank him. He saved our lives."

"This is an animal," Evans counters. "We're limiting contact with people to prevent exposure to diseases while he heals and to prevent the zoo from being swamped by the media. We've had to shut down access to the primate areas of our park for three weeks. Have you any idea what it's been like to keep a lid on this until we could figure out a plan?"

"That's what I'm here to facilitate," Wolf says.

"People, he's not imprisoned—he's quarantined." Vito

says. "Frankly, we're not equipped to deal with this animal. He's wrecked an enclosure—done something like one hundred and fifty thousand dollars in damage. His strength and agility are unlike any we've ever experienced. He's injured staff."

Wolf interrupts. "My backers are prepared to make a substantial donation to this zoo, one that will stabilize your finances for the next decade."

"Now we're talking," Evans says.

"Doctor Evans, how are you treating him?" Hasselbeck asks.

"With the same standard of care that we give all the animals."

"Doctor Hasselbeck," Wolf asserts persuasively. "We're prepared to make a donation to the North American Primate Research Organization that will, frankly, put you on the map. We're also prepared to roll you out as the man who discovered Big Foot. We're talking history here, Doctor Hasselbeck."

"Mr. Two-Moons, we're prepared to invest heavily in your town's infrastructure and in social support for the tribe. We know that your community has been hard hit by flooding and the downturn in the economy."

"Always the same with you people," Two-Moons said. "In America, what you can't take, you buy. But what you're looking to buy, I cannot sell."

"I can't accept this either," Hasselbeck said. "This Big Foot saved the people I love. He could only do such a thing if he was, somehow, human. I'm with the Shaman."

"You're bringing the wrath of the Thunderbird upon yourselves," Two-Moons stated calmly.

"He saved our lives," Marianna added quietly.

I heard Wolf sigh. "Respectfully, I don't think that you fully understand. The potential of this creature is enormous."

"The potential of every person is infinite," Two-Moons responded, "when free to live their lives."

"Don't give us the Shaman crap," Evans snaps angrily. "You need to stop the demonstrations in front. Have you considered the family of the man he killed? This isn't some benevolent, peaceful, forest creature."

"He saved our family!"

"We don't really know what happened on that bluff, do we? All we know is that Clint Norwood is a dead Big Foot hunter."

"That lunatic, Norwood, wasn't a member of our organization." Hasselbeck said incredulously. "He shot me!"

"The bullet went through your shoulder. Maybe your girlfriend here shot you."

I could hear scuffling, angry shouts, pushing and shoving. A chair hit the ground hard.

"Get the hell out of my zoo, you fringe kook!" Evans shouted.

"People," Wolf said calmly, "let's focus on reality—on what we know. Doctor Hasselbeck, do you have any information that elevates this creature to human status? If so, please disclose that now."

"You have my statements. You've got Marianna's statement. It's clear as day."

"The fact of the matter is—and you both have to consider the reality of the situation—that this Big Foot is in the custody of the state. Yes, he's intelligent. Yes, he's extraordinary but..."

"He's lived his entire existence in the wild," Hasselbeck shouted. "He and his kind have successfully defeated all of our attempts to trap, hunt, or lure them from the shadows for decades. This one, for reasons we don't understand, risked his life for a disabled child and his mother. And you show up here to buy him as though he were some sort of product?"

"Okay," Wolf said. "Since you've gone there, imagine, if you will, how we can use this species to better the lives of people, to test drugs and medications. We would no longer have to test new drugs on fully human subjects. His genetic make-up is ninety-nine percent aligned with ours."

"Jesus," Hasselbeck sighed. "You want to turn our closest living relatives over to Pharma and make them Guinea Pigs."

"We could clone these animals for their organs. We could..."

"You're a monster," Marianna interrupted.

I heard a fist pound the table. "Progress always means tough decisions. And they're not always pretty!" It was Wolf again.

"You said he's ninety-nine percent us!" Hasselbeck shouted.

"That one percent is a bitch, isn't it?" Evans answered.

"Look, I can assure you that my backers can assure financial stability for all of you. You three have absolutely no legal standing in any of this and I can say with certainty that the federal government will turn the creature over to the people I represent."

"I thought you were from the federal government," Hasselbeck said loudly. "Who and what are you, really?"

"I am reality, Hasselbeck."

"You think you know the world," Two-Moons said. "But you don't."

"I'm going to end our conversation—for now. Dr. Evans will escort you out of the facility," Wolf said firmly. "I ask you to consider what I've said. We all want to do the right thing. Thanks."

Doors were opened and closed, footsteps receded. A few minutes later, I heard Evans walking in the hallway outside my cell.

"Are they off the property?" Wolf said

"Yeah," Evans answered. "Those people just don't get it."

"They have no legal standing, but they do have the ability to make trouble," Wolf responded. "They have to be dealt with. When the Shaman shows up to chant tomorrow, I'll have our security team deal with him. But let me ask you, do you have any idea about the nature of the creature's relationship with these people?"

"This animal is actually terrifying. You can sense his intellect and he's just human enough to give you the creeps."

"But somehow, Hasselbeck and his woman feel they've got a connection to him."

"I don't know how. I can't wait to get *it* out of here."

"I agree. But arranging secure, secret transportation out of here is taking time. This isn't like moving a race horse to another track," Wolf said. "And we still don't have another location nailed down."

"Please push whoever you have to push. Oh—the MRI machine is being shipped it should be here in a day or two. Getting a look at his organs should be fascinating.

"I agree. I want those images. But first," Wolf said, "I want to see him myself."

"I wouldn't advise that. He's already injured Doctor…"

"Let me see him. You say he's secured?"

"We've added more chains."

"Good. Now get the keys."

A few minutes later, Adolphus Wolf walked into my cell flanked by Orenstein and his aide, both carrying dart guns. The man behind the flames was one of the more impressive humans I've ever seen—well over six feet tall, muscular, with light hair and blue eyes.

"I am Adolphus Wolf," he said.

I could give an elk's fat ass, I wanted to say, but couldn't.

"You smell and you're hairy. But somehow, you've managed to inspire loyalty in a few, stupid people. How did that happen?"

I glared at him.

"Doctor Orenstein, have you seen any indications of higher-level thinking in this animal?"

Orenstein kept the dart gun focused on me. "No. He's just another member of the primate family."

I lunged at Orenstein, knowing full well that the chains would hold me back. Orenstein and the aide nearly fled the room.

Wolf never flinched. "Thank you, Doctor. You've confirmed what I suspected."

Perspiration dotted Orenstein's face. "What do you mean?"

"He understood what you said." Wolf starred at me ruthlessly. "Didn't you, my hairy friend?"

My eyes burned into his.

"Oh, Doctor," he turned to face Orenstein, "if you lie to me again, I'll have his chains removed." He smiled at me. "And then I'll throw you in here with him."

Chapter Thirty-Six

I AWAKE TO a torrent of water. Orenstein's toady aide is spraying me with cold water from an enormous hose.

"Cleaning you up for your big examination in the MRI machine, Big Foot. We need you looking good."

My women always thought that I looked fine, you puny, naked monkey. If I could, I'd stick that hose up your nose and blast your brains out of the back of your head.

I spit some water back at him. Then I grab a handful of wet, stinging sand and fling it into his face. He runs out of the room in agony.

Another lovely day has begun here at the county zoo.

Adolphus Wolf peers through the door slot. "Throwing sand on those smaller than you, I see. Aren't you the beach-bully?"

Wolf swaggers about the building, barking orders at the staff. "Prepare the drugs!" I hear the staff running down the hall, lining up behind the door.

I'm going to have to deal with Wolf, one way or another.

He laughs through the door slot. "I want you to know that we stopped your Shaman friend from protesting in front of the zoo this morning. My security people gave him quite a beating."

I charged the door, enraged. Damn these chains! I put all my energy into pulling on one of them.

"Orenstein, load the sedatives—now!" Wolf shouts.

I rip one heavy chain from the wall. I have a weapon!

Wolf, Orenstein and several security men dash through the door. I whip the loose chain at Wolf's head but he ducks under it and rushes toward me. Arrogant bastard thinks he can bring me down! I kick him backwards and he slides into the wet sand on the floor.

"Ruined my suit, you ugly ape!"

Orenstein fires the dart gun.

I fall to the floor, head spinning. Wolf stands over me. As I lose consciousness, he whispers in my ear. "You can't win." Then he kicks me.

White walls surround me when I regain consciousness. I can barely breathe and I can't move. Their drugs have immobilized me. The machine makes a ceaselessly pounding noise. I scream, but no sound comes out.

Wolf and his minions control every aspect of my life. I, Sasquatch am being reduced to the level of a lab animal. They've taken samples of my tissue. Now they're imaging my body with a machine.

I pray for death, but death eludes me. Once again, I pass out.

I awake on the floor of my enclosure, finally able to move my arms, but chained again. I look at the door and see Wolf's eyes staring at me through the narrow slit.

"You're magnificent," he says. "You have the largest brain of any primate. The experts tell me that you also possess some unusual cerebral structures seen nowhere else in the animal kingdom. I'm betting that these structures allow you to communicate directly with others, brain to brain."

I throw the food dish and it smacks into the viewing slot in the door.

"Good throw! Power and accuracy—this is how you kill your prey isn't it?

I glare at his eyes.

"Know that by time we're finished with you, we'll expose all of your secrets and use them for our benefit. That's why our species is better than yours. That's why we've dominated the planet and pushed your kind to the edge of extinction."

He slides the viewing panel shut.

I awake to hear shouting in the halls.

"The son-of-a-bitch brought a priest and a rabbi with him!"

"They're getting crafty," Wolf responds bitterly. "We can't oppress him with representatives of mainstream religions surrounding him and a television crew filming. I want the media off park property!"

"What do we do now?" Evans asks.

"I'll go out and deal with the media. We need to keep a lid on this until tomorrow. We move him at dawn."

I need some way of signaling to others that I'm here. I pound the walls with my fists and scream. *"WHAAA!"*

My voice is coming back!

"WHAAAAAA!"

"Holy shit," Wolf shouts. "Shut him up!"

Once again, they burst through the door.

"WHAAAAAA!"

Once again, a drug dart drops me to the floor.

I wake up to blinding white lights. I'm strapped to a gurney. Men with masks over their faces and armed with dart guns are escorting other men who are pushing me down the hallway.

I exhale. *"Houff!"* I want them to know that I'm awake.

"Crap! He revived," someone says.

"Dart him in the neck if you have to," Wolf commands, "but keep moving."

I hear a chopping sound coming in from outside; they're pushing me toward the exit. I will soon be outside for the first time in weeks. The promise of breathing in real air from my forest is almost intoxicating.

The plan is to put me in an air machine and take me from my lands, my people, and everything I have ever known.

Filled with despair, I resolve to break free and crash the air machine. Forgive me, Christopher, I know that this will likely kill others and even myself, but I don't see any alternatives. At least my death will be useful if Wolf is on the air ship and dies with me.

I am outside! I can see the first dim light of dawn in the eastern sky. I message Shattuck the Gray. *"They have me in the zoo and they're taking me away in an air machine!"*

"We thought you were dead. What has happened?" Shattuck was getting my messages!

"They've drugged me and made me a prisoner. They plan to take me from our lands and treat me like an animal."

"NOOOO!" he screams in my mind. "They will pay for this!"

I hear wailing noises from police car sirens coming closer to the sounds from the air machine. I guess that they're taking no chances. The armies of human society have arrived to insure my removal.

Then something changes.

"What the..."

"Get out of our way!" Wolf shouts. "We're moving this primate now."

"No, you're not."

I look to my right and see Jack LaHood and several deputies. The police are surrounding the air ship—and Wolf's men.

"You're interfering with our affairs, Sheriff. Get off park property."

"I'm doing my job, you arrogant son-of-a-bitch."

"What the hell are you talking about?" Wolf shouts over the chopping noise from the blades of the sky machine.

"I'm charging this Big Foot with felony crimes," LaHood shouts back. "I have a bench warrant issued by Judge Holland."

"No! You're not pulling this bullshit stunt!" Wolf shouts. "We're moving him now!"

LaHood drew his gun. Wolf and his men stood stunned as the deputies drew theirs as well.

LaHood stood tall and glared at Wolf. "You're just a BS artist in a nice suit, but you brought darts to a gun fight. So, you try to stop me from executin' this warrant and so help me God, you won't live to see the sun rise, punk."

Hasselbeck got out of the back seat of LaHood's cruiser, grinning. "Good morning, Adolphus."

Chapter Thirty-Seven

"YOU HAVE A right to remain silent," Hasselbeck whispers to me. His arm is still in a sling and his face still carries the remains of the violence from a month ago. "Don't say anything to LaHood or the Judge."

I glare at him and he nervously slides closer to the door to the van, protecting his left shoulder.

The notion that humans believe that there is a right to remain silent is bitterly ironic to me. I still cannot speak and I'm still woozy. I may puke from all the drugs they've forced into me. Being crammed into the backseat of a police van, handcuffed, isn't helping. Even worse, the vehicle keeps bottoming out on the road due to my weight as we drive to the Deception Falls Court House. The deputy in the front passenger seat, shaking in terror, has a shot gun pointed at me. The deputy driving looks pretty freaked out, too.

If I vomit all over everyone in the van, will they open fire?

"We're going to help you," Hasselbeck whispers again. "We have a plan."

Yeah, and so far, this is a great plan, Hasselbeck. I'm under arrest and looking down the barrel of a shotgun. Perhaps this is a step up for a zoo animal in human culture but not really the improvement in my situation that I was hoping for.

"LaHood's going to charge you with crimes. The Judge will set bail. We're betting that the bail will be low enough that we can bail you out. Then, LaHood will just let you walk out the front door of police headquarters."

We get to the courthouse just after dawn. The deputies surround the vehicle as I exit. The leg shackles that LaHood's people attached seem even stronger than the ones the zoo used.

"Keep calm," LaHood says quietly. "We're tryin' to help you."

Hasselbeck throws a blanket over my head and I am steered into the building. When the blanket is removed, I am facing the black-robed Judge Holland. We stare at each other for what seems like an eternity.

"Sheriff LaHood, you never cease to amaze me," Judge Holland said, unable to take her eyes off me. "Even though I listened to that recording and prepared for this moment, I am still in awe."

"He is impressive, Your Honor," LaHood says.

"It now occurs to me," the Judge says, "that Deception Falls is really properly named. This is indeed the place where deceptions fall."

LaHood nodded. "I couldn't agree more."

The court clerk interrupts their conversation. "All rise! The Court of Deception Falls is in session. The Honorable and Right, M. J. Holland presides."

"Okay," she says. "We are arraigning this...this..."

"Big Foot," Hasselbeck says. "This fellow is a Big Foot."

"Indeed." she answers. "What's your job title again, Doctor Hasselbeck?"

"Cryptozoologist."

"Your Honor," a young woman in a business suit standing next to LaHood says. "Sheriff Jack LaHood has... well...instructed the People to bring one count of Man Slaughter, Assault, Criminal Mischief and other lesser, but related crimes, against this Big Foot. This is a return on a warrant. The matter before the court is to make arrangements for further proceedings, assign or determine counsel, consider a plea, and set bail."

LaHood cleared his throat. "The State Penal Law is, as Your Honor is well aware, quite clear, that the police are obligated to charge *all* persons who break the law, regardless of their race, class, gender or social status."

"The court is aware of the expectations of the police, Sheriff."

"And to fulfill my legal obligation, I had to remove to the defendant from the Cascadia County Zoo." LaHood then gave Hasselbeck a wry smile.

A man in a suit carrying a brief case enters quickly from the rear of the room and stands next to me, mouth agape. "Holy shit!"

"Indeed, counselor. Did you get where we are here?"

"I heard the People as I came in, Your Honor, but..."

"But what?"

"I'm not sure that I can represent a non-human." He sees me glaring at him. "No offense...sir."

Adolphus Wolf is sitting in the rear of the court room. "He's right!"

"Who are you?" Judge Holland asked.

"Adolphus Wolf. I represent a group of interested parties who..."

"Do you represent this Big Foot?"

"Well, no. I represent people who..."

"Then you will silence yourself or I will have the deputies remove you. You're not a party to these proceedings."

"This isn't a person!" Wolf screams. "It's an animal. This is absurd and these people are trying to use *human* criminal charges against a primate to remove the property of the Cascadia County Zoo!"

"Remove this man," Holland says loudly. LaHood makes eye contact with his deputies and they shove Wolf toward the door.

"I'll be back! I'm going to the Governor!" Wolf shouts. Then the door slams shut.

"He may have a point," The woman who represents The People says plainly. "I'm not sure that we can do this. I don't know if the law's ever gone here."

LaHood clears his throat. "Your Honor, Washington State's criminal laws state that a person breaks the law when he or she commits certain acts deemed to be criminal by the legislature. The legislature never specified that a *person* can only be a human being."

Holland looks at me closely. "The possibility of this situation may never have occurred to them."

Hasselbeck steps forward. "If I may, Your Honor, non-living entities—such as corporations—have been legally defined as *persons*. This entity's DNA has been analyzed and I'm advised that ninety-nine percent of his DNA matches human DNA."

The judge nodded. "That may be so, Mr. Hasselbeck, but the issue for me is this fellow's mental capacity, ability to reason and act based on cognition. An animal may exhibit behavior that results in human harm or impact, but we do not generally view that behavior as criminal or possibly criminal. I think I have to determine the *intent* of this being."

Hasselbeck held up his phone. "The evidence is in the recording."

"It may be," she said. "But, as I told you, I need to ask some questions. I cannot rely on a cell phone recording. I have to assess his intent." She focused on me again. "This is the most remarkable day of my legal career. Frankly, the most remarkable day of my life." She pointed at me. "Sir, I listened to a cellphone-recorded conversation that I have reason to believe you took part in. I can see that you were recently wounded in the throat. Have you the ability now to speak?"

I tried to respond but couldn't form proper human words. I lifted my cuffed hands and pointed to my throat and growled. "Nah yut."

The attorney standing next to me looked at me in amazement. "Your Honor, my client seems to have said 'Not yet'." I nodded to him.

The judge nodded. "Very good. I need to ask you if you know this man here, Doctor Joseph Hasselbeck."

I looked at Hasselbeck and nodded. Damn fool smiled at me.

"Without discussing any potential crimes—that's a different phase of the proceedings—did you have a conversation with him a few weeks ago on a snowy day in the woods?"

I nodded.

"You were angry with this man, weren't you?"

I looked at Hasselbeck and nodded.

"You considered harming him, didn't you?"

I looked at Hasselbeck, then returned my attention to the judge, feeling a bit guilty.

She took her glasses off and put them on the table. "But then you decided not to harm him. You made this decision because he revealed to you that he loves the same people that you do. Is that correct?"

"Yef."

Holland nodded. "The court has assessed this...Big Foot. Based on what I heard on the recording in chambers and what the Big Foot has confirmed with primitive language and non-verbal communications here in court, I believe that this primate is in fact, a 'person'. He is a person because he acts with a purpose and intent. He even makes mistakes born of emotions—just as we do. And, he has the capacity for anger and love, just as we do. It is for these reasons that he may—and I emphasize 'may' because the People must prove crimes beyond a reasonable doubt—have intentionally damaged several thousand dollars-worth of property belonging to Doctor Joseph Hasselbeck. I am not convinced that the statements made on the recording necessarily connect this person to other, more serious potential crimes. However, it is clear that the statements indicate the possibility that this person committed assault and criminal mischief. Counselor, how does your client plead?"

"Huh?" my attorney said.

The Judge leaned forward. "Counselor, do you intend to enter a plea on behalf of your client?"

I glared at him.

"I'm entering a plea of *Not Guilty*."

"Very well, then. I am prepared to set bail to insure his return to court to face further proceedings."

"The People ask for bail in the amount of ten thousand dollars, Your Honor."

Judge Holland turned to my attorney. "Counselor?"

"Seems a little high, Your Honor. He has no priors."

Everybody burst out laughing but I didn't know why.

The judge spoke to me directly. "Sir, do you have a name?"

I nodded. "*Ciatqoqua...Sasqua...Sasquatch.*"

Chapter Thirty-Eight

I SAT IN A JAIL cell in the basement of Police Head-quarters, looking at Hasselbeck and Mongo. They brought me fresh salmon and some plants from my domain and watched me eat, saying nothing. It was the best I'd felt in weeks, even though I was still in captivity.

"Two-Moons is taking up a collection to bail you out," Hasselbeck said. "LaHood says that once he has the bail money, he will release you." Then he smiled wryly, "As long as you promise to make your next court appear-ance."

I nodded in agreement. We both understood that I was going to bolt into the woods the minute the cuffs were off. And I wouldn't be coming back.

He leaned against the bars. "I'm sorry for what you've been through. I honestly thought that the people at the zoo would release you once you recovered. The Cascadia County Zoo touts its *Recover and Release Program* for injured wildlife.

They didn't mean this particular variety of wildlife, Hasselbeck.

"Adolphus Wolf is a monster."

I gave him a look that said, *No shit*.

He leaned in closer and whispered. "The Shaman showed me what Christopher said. I read every word. We're calling it *The Book of Christopher, As Told by His Brother, Sasquatch*." His eyes misted. "The Shaman had his nephew type them into a manuscript."

The Shaman's nephew, Whale Shit, continues to impress me. Who knew he could type?

"Christopher really spoke those words to you?"

I looked at him incredulously. Do you think that dominant males have time to dream up spiritual manuscripts? I nodded. "Yef."

"You know what I think?"

No, but I was sure that he was about to tell me.

"We spend so much of our lives wandering the planet, looking for discoveries. Yet we don't see the miracles happening right in front of our eyes."

I nodded.

"My friends at the television network have connected me to a courageous publisher in New York. Looks like we're going to publish the book."

"I'm gonna get you more salmon," Mongo said, turning to leave. Then Rachel, on crutches, ambled in. She stopped a few feet in front of the bars, dumbstruck. Mongo turned to me. "You know Rachel, don't you?"

"Yef."

Rachel couldn't take her eyes off me. "My God, you're beautiful."

I didn't know how to respond to that.

"You saved my life," she said.

Then Marianna and Christopher turned the corner and stood next to her.

"Why?" Rachel asked. "I understand now that we were annoying you. We were interfering with your business, your world. Yet you stopped a huge brown bear from killing me. Why did you save my life?"

I couldn't form the words. Anyway, it was hard to explain. I pointed at Christopher. "Fuh Chrispufur."

I kneeled down and extended my hand out as far as I could between the bars and touched Christopher's hand. Once again, I felt his peaceful energy and received his thoughts.

"Mommy and Joseph are helping me. This would never have been possible without you. When you are freed, you must run into the woods and never come back."

"To do that, I must know that you are free from silence."

Later that night, LaHood and his men woke me up by jingling some keys. "The Shaman bailed you out. We're gonna cuff you, walk you upstairs, un-cuff you, and let you walk outta' here."

My heart was racing as he opened the cell door.

LaHood smirked. "You gotta promise to make your court appearance next Wednesday."

I nodded and held out my hands so he could cuff me. We walked quickly up the stairs to the front desk. Two-Moons stood next to Whale-Shit, signing some papers, smiling at the desk officer. He turned to me. "Spring is in the air, my brother. It's a good night for a walk in the woods." They walked with me out of the building and stood on the steps, watching me.

LaHood un-cuffed me and looked me in the eye. "Get outta here."

I turned and walked quickly through the glass doors and into a starlit night. The chilly night air was exhilarating. I ran down the steps and could see the forest, no more than a few hundred feet away. All I had to do was cross the road and I would be free.

A dart hit me in the thigh and I fell to the floor.

Cars and vans swooped in from every direction. Men who looked like soldiers emerged from the cars. More streamed from out of the woods and from behind the building. They were armed with long guns that I'd never seen before.

I yanked the dart out of my leg and kept moving toward the woods, limping.

I heard the voice of that maniac, Adolphus Wolf. "We prefer to take him alive."

"What the hell is this?" LaHood shouted.

"Get out of my way or we'll shoot!"

"Hit 'em again!" someone shouted.

Another dart struck me in the shoulder. I pulled this one out and hurled it at a soldier. When it embedded in his chest, he screamed in agony. I turned to see another soldier running up the steps toward LaHood. Wolf followed him, holding a document. "We're taking this animal into state custody by order of the Governor!" he shouted.

"This is my town, you bastards!" LaHood screamed. "The man's freed on bail!"

My head was spinning and I felt as though I'd lose consciousness. When a soldier grabbed my arm. I picked him up and tossed him onto the roof of a nearby car. He landed with a loud crunch, as the roof caved under the force of his landing.

"Run C'iatqo!" I heard Two-Moons shout.

"Get down, old man, or we'll shoot!"

"Run C'iatqo! Run!"

"He's got a club!"

"Drop him!" someone shouted.

I heard gunfire and turned to see Two-Moons rolling down the steps. His nephew ran after him, screaming. "No!"

Then they shot him, too.

I ran back toward Two-Moons, tossing soldiers out of my way. *"WAHOOOO!"* One grabbed the hair on my back. I turned and slammed my fist down on his helmet; he crumpled to the ground.

"Dart him again!"

I felt two more darts hit me in the back as I caught a glimpse of a soldier slamming the butt of a rifle into LaHood's jaw, dropping him to the ground.

I fell to my knees over Two-Moons. *"WAHHH!"*

Another soldier ran at me. I back-handed him and heard his jaw snap out of its socket before he tumbled down the steps.

Then I heard an explosion and found myself covered in thick netting that tightened and pulled me down. I crawled to where Two-Moons lay. Blood poured from the wounds in his chest. "Touch my hands, my brother."

I held his hands through the netting and looked into his eyes. *"Nuwo!"* I moaned.

"It's not your fault, my brother." Peace filled his eyes. "Hold on to what is good, even if it is a handful of earth. Hold on to what you love, even if it is a tree which stands by itself. Hold on to life, even when it is easier to let go. Hold on to my hand, even as I pass away from you."

I looked up and saw Adolphus Wolf looming over me. Then I felt the Shaman's grip loosening on my hands. Two-Moons looked up into the night sky. "The stars are beautiful my brother, but the waters rise...the waters rise."

Chapter Thirty-Nine

I AM ONCE AGAIN held in the cold whiteness of the examination room at the county zoo. Bright lights pierce my eyes, and I am surrounded by the whirling sound of electronic machines.

Then I hear the pounding of the tube machine.

I want to break free, but I'm strapped to a flat gurney. *"WAAAAAH!"*

The pounding stops.

"He's a freak of nature," someone says. "We've given him more drugs than you'd give a bull elephant and still he wakes up."

"My people want a better image of his frontal lobe," Wolf said. "We're into this animal for a fortune. Increase his drip if you have to. Remember, he's killed two officers."

"You killed a Shaman and his nephew, Wolf. Your day is coming." Then, the pounding noise from the machine started again.

I wake in a chair, completely restrained. My head is held in place by metal clamps so that I'm forced to look at a television screen of some sort. Electrodes are imbedded into my skull and I can feel a tangle of wires all around me. The wires connect to more electronics, more machines.

I, Sasquatch, have become an electronic prisoner.

They are peering into my mind. These monsters seek to rip everything from me. Taking my freedom wasn't enough. Tearing me from my people and my land wasn't enough. Killing my friends in cold blood wasn't enough.

Now they want my mind.

Colors flash in front of my eyes.

"He can see colors," a woman says. "He's got amazing visual capabilities."

Then the lights dim. I'm presented with a dim image of a hunter in in the woods, wearing clothes to make him blend in with his surroundings.

"Yep. He's got vision that's way better than ours. I'd have to run the algorithms to give you some numbers, but he sees us long before we see him."

Wolf leans in and smiles at me. "This is why you've always stayed hidden. You see us coming from miles away." He turned to the female. "If we could replicate his visual system, the military implications would be huge."

"I'm thinking that his auditory centers are the envy of the primate world," the woman says. "He's amazing."

Wolf is staring at me, smiling. "I agree. Everyone should own one."

I feel more drugs pushed through needles into my arms and I black out. I wake up in the same place, the television screen on. I am presented with images of humans working, caring for children, and participating in athletic events. The random images mean little to me.

Then the images change.

I am presented with visions from hell. Humans lie dead on a battle field. Burning buildings are reduced to ruins. A crying child clings to her dead mother. Young men with severed limbs lie dead in a muddy hole in the ground, eyes starring lifelessly into eternity.

"WAAAAH!"

Once again, I am plunged into darkness. But now my sleep is filled with bad dreams and images of horror and carnage. I awake. I am chained to Tang's cement tree outside.

Am I really outside? I look up and see stars. Then everything fades to black.

Shattuck the Gray stands before me.

"I told you to forget about the boy and disappear into the shadows. And you wouldn't listen."

"I could not abandon the boy."

"His own people abandoned him. His own people poisoned and shunned him."

"I could not."

"Look at their world. The images they showed you are what they are about. They're so busy destroying the earth that they don't see their own extinction looming on the horizon."

"If I turned my back on him, more light would leave the world."

"You saw the images. The elders have always known what the humans were capable of doing. They've desecrated their world. They've blown out their own candles."

"The child can bring them out of their darkness. Maybe his words can help us leave the shadows."

"You've been driven to this madness by the loss of your son. Now captivity has stolen your mind."

"This child has absorbed the worst of humanity and yet speaks only of love and kindness. He has opened a new world where hope is possible."

"You're as naïve as I was over a hundred years ago. Only now do I understand my father's wisdom. Massacre the humans. Inflict an atrocity upon them that they will never forget so that they never return to our lands. That is why he initiated the slaughter."

"And look what that caused our native brothers and sisters."

"They would have been victimized anyway. It is what these monsters do. We will make them fear our kind and avoid our lands so that they never bother us again. If we can no longer keep our world secret, then we will fill the humans with dread. We will kill them all."

"Do not do this, my elder. Violence does not cure violence."

"We are coming."

Once again, I wake to the stark whiteness. Once again, I am strapped to a table. I try to sit up, but the effort is useless.

"I wanted to have some time alone with you," Wolf says. "I want you to understand."

I hear him walking around me. Come closer, you blue-eyed bastard. What I would give for the chance to clutch your throat, to watch your face turn red, then purple, then lifeless white.

"We are ancient enemies, you and I. We both know that. We've been at war since time began. I can say that confidently because your kind and my kind are the only animals that understand the passage of time. This is what we share."

Come closer, Wolf. And we will share eternity together.

"Do you know that the first story ever written in English is about a clash between one of your ancestor's and one of mine?"

I glare at him.

"Mine won. Now look to your left."

I turn to see the dead body of Tang, the Orangutan, on the gurney next to me.

"WAAAH! WAAAH!"

"No one can hear your screams. No one heard his. Tang was put down by the authorities here because they had no room for him. Just like that." He snapped his fingers. "They need his space for you."

I growl and stare at him with murderous intent.

"The public relations folks who work with the people I work with have made an interesting decision. They've decided to announce your existence. We are putting you on display."

I fought against the restraints, clutching for Wolf. Forgive me, Christopher, I need only to kill one more man.

"I'm inclined to secrecy. I'd prefer to pay off those who need paying off, keep a lid on all of this and issue denials. Issue enough denials and people will just move along to the next story." He took out a hand gun. "I've been trained in secrecy. Other men are trained in more conventional warfare. My expertise, however, is killing in silence." He screwed a device onto the end of his gun. "I could kill you with this and no one would hear the gun shot." He leaned over my head and held the gun against my skull.

I looked him in the eyes.

"Remarkable. You don't fear death. That is something else that we share." He unscrewed the device and put the gun back in his jacket. "I will go along with this plan because there is a genius to it." He walked over to Tang's body. "The people I really work for understand that people today have short attention spans. They spend their days moving from one stimulation to the next." Wolf raised his palms, as though revealing a great secret. "But they never really stop to look at what is going on around them. Never stop to analyze how they're being deceived, or manipulated." He held his hands together, as though in prayer. "Until one day, they have surrendered everything to us." He paused and pointed at Tang. "Once upon a time, this fellow was an amazing discovery. Now, he's just a dead primate."

"WAAAAH!"

"Now, it is time for you and your kind to surrender. We are going to announce to the world that I, Adolphus Wolf, have discovered and captured the mighty Sasquatch. For a while, you'll be an attraction. People will be amazed by you. Then, they will move on. By then, we will study you and, eventually, take every secret from you that we can." He looked at me coldly. "For whatever purposes we choose."

Rage burned in my heart. I wanted to rip his guts out.

"We're going to display you in chains, the way a monster should be displayed. 'Come see the terrifying Sasquatch'. We're going to de-mystify you and de-humanize you. Within no time, you'll be just another animal."

Chapter Forty

THE OPENING DAY of my exhibit broke crisp and blue. The Cascadia County Zoo was buzzing with activity. I could hear the chopping sound of the air machine that delivered me to this prison, weeks ago.

At least I was outside. My mind was re-connecting to the forest just beyond the zoo.

They drugged me, as usual, and moved me to Tang's old enclosure. Chains tethered me to his ridiculous artificial tree. I noticed that they raised the fences another twenty feet. Adolphus Wolf wasn't taking any chances with his prize.

An enormous, black mesh cloth covered the entire enclosure. I could see through it, somewhat.

I could hear commanders giving orders to security guards. Large trucks were moving in and out; I could see workers finishing the construction of a grandstand facing my cage. To my right, I saw that a podium had been erected. The men were talking about how the Governor would run the proceedings from it.

"The scrim comes off the enclosure when the Governor gives the signal," one man told another man.

"Do we know how this animal will react when he sees all the people looking at him?"

"I'm more worried about what the people will do when they see him. They may rush the enclosure. That's why we need more security up front."

I looked up into the blue sky and saw the Thunderbird circling.

Because I was finally outside, my mind connected to my people. Males were fashioning clubs. Females were gathering rocks. They were merging nearby, moving slowly toward the zoo, undetected. The grim visage of Shattuck the Gray burned in mind.

"I feel your presence, Gray One. There will be too many of them here. Please don't do what you're planning to do."

"It doesn't matter how many are there. They will all die."

"You must not do this. There is no point in another massacre."

"Yes, there is."

People began filling the grandstand. Music blasted throughout the zoo. Another sky machine landed.

"The Governor's here," a male voice shouted into a handheld device.

"Where's Adolphus?" another asked.

"I'm in here."

I turned to see Wolf standing by the entrance to the enclosure. I ran toward him, prepared to rip him to pieces, but the chains snapped tight before I could get within ten feet.

He stood smiling. "We've tested the security system a dozen times, my friend. You've no hope of escape. However, I invite you to growl and howl and spit and terrify everyone here. Smelly, squalid, shocking Sasquatch! What theatre."

Wolf was a dead man and didn't know it. *"WAAAAH!"*

I could feel the crowd stir beyond the scrim.

Far above me, the Thunderbird circled.

"The zoo is overflowing with thousands of people. This is going to fabulous," Wolf smirked. Then he exited the enclosure.

"Sasquatch, Mommy and I are here with Joey." Christopher messaged me. "We've brought signs protesting what they've done to you. Mongo and Joey plan to set you free."

"Ladies and gentlemen, I am Governor Andrew Collins. Welcome to one of the greatest days in the history of the great state of Washington…"

"Oh, God, no. Christopher, get out of here. My people are coming. There's going to be a massacre. I'm chained to a cement tree. I can't protect you from what's going to happen."

"But there are soldiers and helicopters and the Governor's security team. These men have guns."

"They don't understand how we fight, Christopher. You can't shoot what you can't see. My elders intend to kill everyone here."

"They have television cameras."

"They're going to put the slaughter of hundreds on television! You have to tell your mother."

"I can't talk."

"You have to! I can't stop this! I'm chained."

"We are here, Sasquatch," Shattuck messaged, "and we are going to light the flames that will consume these monsters once and for all."

"No! Do not do this, Shattuck! These humans don't understand what they're doing."

"And now," Governor Collins announced, "behold the mighty Sasquatch, Lord of the Dark Woods!"

The security men pulled some cords and the scrim fell down around the enclosure. The crowd rose with a collective gasp.

Above me, the Thunderbird cried.

"WAAAAH!" I ran toward the crowd to warn them, but the chains pulled tight. Once again, the crowd gasped, recoiling in fear and amazement.

"Sasquatch," Christopher said. "It's time to pray."

"I cannot save them. I cannot save you. I am alone."

"You have never been alone. I've brought you a rose. Pray."

I looked, in silence, at the crowd standing in the bleachers before me. They were just people, and they were all going to die unless I did something. I bowed my head and thought of the rose.

"Blessed are those who protect the weak, they shall be given the sky." I looked for my people in the crowd but couldn't find them. "The sky shelters us all."

"And now," The Governor spoke. "The man who discovered and captured Sasquatch, Mr. Adolphus...."

I looked at the people, some in the eye. "We are all brothers and sisters and we all share the sky. We are all connected through time and blood."

"He's speaking!" someone shouted.

"Sasquatch can speak?" someone else responded.

Hasselbeck waived his arms to get the crowd's attention. He held a huge speaking devise that carried his voice. "Because he's a *person*." Hasselbeck pointed at Wolf. "*That* monster put a *person* in chains."

"Speak again, Sasquatch," Christopher messaged.

My full voice had returned. I looked up to the sky and fell to my knees. The chains held my arms high. "I look to God to stir compassion in my brothers and sisters to see our shared humanity. I ask God for the strength to rise when others would knock me down, to speak when others would impose silence, and to love when others would hate."

"He's praying," someone said.

"He believes in God," someone else said.

The Governor turned to Wolf. "What the hell is this?"

"It's an accident," he stammered. Wolf glared at me and reached for his gun.

Mongo held a giant pair of bolt clips over his head and shouted, "Free the Squatch!"

"We're Americans," Marianna shouted. "We don't do this to people. Free Sasquatch!"

Mongo stood tall. "Free the Squatch! Free the Squatch!"

The television cameras filmed as the crowd rushed the enclosure, pushing against the gate, chanting, "Free the Squatch! Free the Squatch!" The soldiers and the Governor's security team tried to hold the stampeding crowd back but were overwhelmed.

"Get the Governor out of here!" a security officer ordered.

"No!" Wolf shouted. "This wasn't meant to happen!"

The crowd surged with such force that the ground shook. The gate gave way, and the throng spilled into enclosure. I saw Jack LaHood running toward the podium to intercept Wolf. The security team rushed the Governor toward the helicopter, shoving protestors out of the way.

People circled me, reaching out and patting my fur. The crowd surged and lifted me off my feet. Mongo snapped the chains with the bolt clipper. "You're free, Squatch. Run for the hills."

"Where are Christopher and Marianna?" I shouted. "You need to get them out of here!"

A group of people grabbed my chains and began pulling the cement tree off its moorings. The tree was swaying, almost like a real tree. "Tear it down!" a woman shouted.

The crowd joined the woman and chanted, "Tear it down! Tear it down!"

"Hasselbeck," LaHood shouted. "Get Marianna and Christopher outa here!"

Then people began falling to the ground, bleeding.

"It's Wolf," Hasselbeck screamed. "He's shooting innocent people to try to stop them from freeing Squatch! He's gone mad!"

A round burned through the skin of my arm; I fell to the floor as people began fleeing in terror. People were being trampled. The security guards launched tear gas into the crowd, fueling the panic. Things had spiraled out of control.

I got to my feet and saw Wolf charging toward me, enraged, gun at the ready. "Damn you!" He had me in his sights.

"Get down!" LaHood shouted from behind me. "He's mine."

I dropped low and LaHood shot Wolf in the chest. Wolf dropped his gun and fell to his knees. "This can't be happening." He shook his head in disbelief.

A moment later, the cement tree fell, crushing him.

LaHood helped me up. "Get outta here."

Hasselbeck, Marianna, and Christopher somehow found us through the chaos. I touched Christopher's hand for the last time and he handed me the rose.

The Governor's helicopter lifted off and turned to begin its ascent when rocks smashed into it from every direction. The sky machine became unbalanced, tilted sideways, and plummeted back to earth, crashing into another zoo enclosure and exploding into flames.

"Oh my God," LaHood shouted. "The Governor was in that. What happened?"

I shielded my eyes from the explosion. "It's my people. They're attacking. They're going to kill everybody."

A security guard fell to the floor, just outside the gate. Another staggered under an unrelenting assault of rocks. A television camera toppled over and exploded as rocks continued to rain down from high atop the forest trees. The camera operator fled. The woods exploded with the war whoops of dominant males and the pounding of oak clubs.

I turned to Hasselbeck. "Joseph, take Marianna and the child and flee these lands."

Hasselbeck grabbed my shoulder. "Come with us. You're free now."

"I cannot go with you. I must stay here and fight my own kind to save as many of the humans as I can."

"You owe us nothing," he pleaded. "We've killed your loved ones, enslaved you, exploited and tortured you. We've desecrated your world."

"Joseph, a new world is coming. I cannot speak the words that Christopher shared with me and then run into the woods while people are slaughtered. I must *live* the words. My path ends here. Today I overcome my shadow. Today I make my stand. Now go!"

And then I witnessed the miracle that Two-Moons promised: Christopher spoke.

"The sky, Sasquatch." He pointed to heaven. "The sky."

"Yes, little one. We will always share the sky. The blue, blue sky."

Praise for
The Book of Sasquatch

The world needed books like *Atlas Shrugged* until they lost faith in government. I predict that the world will remember *The Book of Sasquatch* as a compelling parable on the noxious patriarchal cultural hegemony pressed on individuals, families, and tribes who still believe in the promise of mystery and the unknown.

—Jack Lyons-Weiler, PhD

Conte slips you into Sasquatch's world and behind his eyes. Sasquatch is at once both primitive and more evolved than the humans hunting him. And Sasquatch is very funny. Observing a small, different boy and his overworked park ranger Mom, he sends out a primal call to remind us that empathy, protection, and dignity still matter. Especially when we, too, are feeling... captured.

— Kim Stagliano Ross, author of
All I Can Handle: I'm No Mother Teresa

Not only is Conte's *The Book of Sasquatch* a page turner, it's a thoughtful commentary on how humanity has been led astray by greed and pride but is still capable of redemption if more people will open their hearts and stand up for what is right.

—Leslie Manookian, director of *The Greater Good*

Conte's *The Book of Sasquatch*, written from a first Sasquatch perspective, is an outsider's tale that resonates with the alienation that lives within so many of us.

—Mark Giuliano, vocalist and song writer for Sons of Ghidorah

Lou Conte is a master storyteller whose wit and charm capture the reader and transport them into a world that delights the imagination. *The Book of Sasquatch* should be read by every high school student in America!

—Dr. Andy McCabe, host of
"Autism with Dr. Andy," HealthyLife.net
and author of *The Gifted One* and
How Women Will Change the World

CPSIA information can be obtained
at www.ICGtesting.com
Printed in the USA
FSHW012045010421
79971FS